Men & Women of Letters

Men & Women of Letters

An Anthology of Short Stories
by Letter Carriers

Edited by John Yewell

Men & Women of Letters
Palo Alto, California

Copyright 1988 by John Yewell

First Printing 1988
Printed in The United States of America

Library of Congress Cataloging in Publication Data

An Anthology of short stories by letter carriers.

(Writers who work ; v. 1)
At Head of title: Men & Women of Letters.
1. Letter carriers' writings, American.   2. Short stories, American.   3. Postal service—Fiction.
I. Yewell, John, 1954–   II. Men & Women of Letters (Publisher)   III. Series.
PS647.L47A84   1988   813'.01'0892383   88–92270
ISBN 0-9621322-0-9

300 S. Montgomery   © 1984 by MERCURY PRESS, INC.
Reprinted from
The Magazine of Fantasy and Science Fiction

Printed By Boyd Printing Company, Albany, New York

Acknowledgments

There are many people to thank for their assistance over the past two years, but chief among them is Vince Bontempi. Vince believed in this book from the very beginning, and never once waivered in his faith and conviction that we would succeed. Without his support, both spiritual and financial, this book would never have happened, and to him I owe more than he will admit.

I would also like to thank the members of my reading committee: Vince, David Watson, Frank Ware, and Al Apfelbaum. Their advice was critical in guiding the selection of stories included here, and I am grateful for their contribution. Thanks also go to Stan Weir at Singlejack Books for his advice and assistance in the production of this book, to Graham Vane, Anita Guzik and Joan Hurst of the California State Association of Letter Carriers for their support, to Lorraine Swerdloff and the *Postal Record* for launching the ship, to Gene O'Neill and Fred Wright for helping to keep the rudder pointed in the right direction, to my friend Paul Haxo for his vision, to Basil Zuniga for helping out, to my branch president John Spencer for his support, to Bil Paul for his help in publicizing the project, to Susan Hemmenway for her help with the cover, to Carl Johnson at Boyd Printing for guiding us so patiently through production, and above all to my wife Joëlle, who kept me sane throughout the last year and whose crazy idea this was in the first place.

John Yewell

Front cover illustration by Ellery Knight

Back cover design by John Yewell

CONTENTS

INTRODUCTION

The goal of *Men & Women of Letters* was to publish the best collection of short stories we could attract; subject matter was not a consideration. We had only two criteria: talent, and membership in the National Association of Letter Carriers. Of the sixteen stories in this collection, only six deal in some way with the Post Office.

In the one year during which we actively solicited manuscripts we received a total of 120 stories from 65 letter carriers in 25 states. Some of these carriers and stories had been published previously. A committee of local postal employees with literary backgrounds helped me in reviewing the submissions. We did our best to be scrupulously fair: I myself submitted a story—under an assumed name—and was turned down by my readers. To this day they do not know which one was mine.

The reader will not fail to notice, however, that although we have "Women" in the title, we do not have one in the table of contents. We did receive nineteen stories from thirteen women writers, and made a special effort to solicit others. I personally regret that no women were published, but it was impossible to give special consideration to any group as such. The relative lack of manuscripts from women is due to the obvious fact that the letter carrier craft is still dominated by men. For a time we considered changing the title of the book, but we hope the second volume of *Men & Women of Letters* will include women letter carrier-writers.

The idea for *Men & Women of Letters* was born in December, 1986. Each year the Post Office's employee magazine, *Postal Life*, publishes a calendar illustrated with artwork by postal employees. Some of that work is quite good. My wife Joëlle was looking at the 1987 calendar and happened to comment that somebody ought to do the same thing for the writers in the Post Office. The title occurred to me in an instant. The book itself took two years.

The choice of the word "Stories"—as opposed to "Fiction"—in our subtitle was deliberate. Our commitment to the best writing precluded having a strong attachment to the distinction—which is often blurred anyway. When a writer begins with the intention of writing fiction he cannot help but write about what he knows. This sometimes lead into autobiography. On the other hand, when a writer *sets out* to write autobiography, the temptation to embellish the facts in the search for truth sometimes leads into fiction. Most of *Men & Women of Letters* is fiction.

An ancillary goal of ours all along has been to raise the self-esteem of our craft. The general public has a very precious, quaint notion of the dedicated, selfless "mailman" braving the elements to see that the mail goes through. Much of that impression is deserved, but the fact remains that carriers, just as other blue-collar workers, are not expected to display any intellectual or creative prowess. The public's expectations become the public's stereotype.

The problems of self-image and public misconceptions are not a postal monopoly. Working people everywhere, whatever the color of their collar, deal in—indeed, rely on—roles and images. But such impressions mislead, and our perceptions of a group have nothing to do with the talents of individuals we have never met.

The power of art overcomes stereotypes. If, the next time you see a carrier making his or her rounds, you wonder what secret talent that person—or any "working" person—may have, then this book will have been a success. We also hope you will enjoy what you read.

With this in mind, it is our intention to publish a series of short story anthologies highlighting the literary talents of people working in various crafts and professions. Here you have volume 1 of the series, Writers Who Work.

John Yewell, October, 1988
San Mateo, California

You must not suppose, because I am a man of letters, that I never tried to earn an honest living.

— George Bernard Shaw

300 S. MONTGOMERY

by

GENE O'NEILL

Moving stiffly, the heavy mist like a fallen cloud: light distorted, images blurred, sounds sharp but dislocated. Strange . . . surreal, yet not really frightening: almost comforting, like a cloak of gauze, soft, protective. Slowly the stiffness eases from limbs, movement smoothing to an effortless glide—Then suddenly, far ahead in the mist, a doorway of light . . . framing a woman, her face clear and distinct, highlighted by a bright beam. . . . A cascade of black hair with a silvery dab in front, high cheek bones polished rose, full lips forming a wide smile . . . Long, graceful fingers making a beckoning gesture—But the door swinging shut. Run! Faster, faster. Hurry, the outstretched hand . . . Heart pounding, lungs gasping. Just another step, now—The light blinks out. At the closed door . . . Pounding furiously, pounding on the cold number 300 . . . No, no, Kay . . . Kay. . . .

"Kay . . ." Neal McCarthy awakened from the dream, his head throbbing with pain. He reached across the bed, his fingers frantically clawing the crumpled sheet. Numbly he stared at the empty half-bed, the undented pillow. "Kay . . ." Then he groaned as the reality dawned: his wife *was* gone.

She had died in the car accident five months ago, coming home from the Christmas party. He closed his eyes and breathed deeply, overcome by his guilt. But he felt her presence, so near, always so near. . . . If only there was a way to reach her—"Jesus!" he whispered hoarsely, "Let go, man, let go." It was only a damn dream. Kay and the number. She *was* gone—and he was so sick.

He forced his eyes open, focusing on the digital clock on the

1

nightstand: 7:10 a.m. The figures blurred as he realized he was going to be late for work. Still, he was unable to move, paralyzed by the sense of his wife's nearness . . . and his pounding head. He had a loose, queasy feeling deep in his gut.

Maybe I'll call in sick, Neal thought, reaching for the phone beside the clock—but his hand halted in midair, halfway to the phone. *No,* he'd called in yesterday . . . and twice last week. Shit, he thought, his hand sagging to the side of the bed.

Then, with an effort of will, Neal sat upright and swung his legs out of bed. Ignoring the fresh wave of nausea, he stood up and stumbled across the room. He steadied himself against the chair and pulled on his postal uniform trousers, the effort sending slivers of pain into his skull. For a moment he remained motionless, afraid he was going to throw up. After several deep breaths the nausea eased, and he shambled into the closet. Unable to find a clean shirt, he returned to the chair and bent over to pick up the wrinkled shirt off the floor. Feeling light-headed and dizzy, he sagged to a kneeling position. Again he breathed slowly and evenly. After a moment he was able to stand. He slipped on the shirt and headed for the kitchen. Jerking open the fridge door, he found a can of Bud. With trembling fingers he popped off the top and drained the beer in two long swallows. As an afterthought he searched through the junk drawer and found two Excedrin. He took them, drinking from the faucet over the sink.

Feeling slightly better, he shaved and left the apartment.

Neal nodded as he rushed past the two clerks smoking on the loading dock behind the main post office. He pushed through the set of swinging freight doors and cut across the main floor, past the rows of parcel post tubs, to the time clock. He felt a glimmer of hope as he punched in and glanced at the carrier supervisor's desk. Only three minutes late. Danberg had his back turned, checking the assignment board.

Maybe I can just ease by, Neal thought hopefully—

But Danberg turned before Neal could sneak by, a scowl etched on his heavy features. "McCarthy, you're late," Danberg said, his high-pitched, nasal voice at odds with his huge frame. He shook his head, disgust replacing the scowl. "Did you sleep in that shirt?"

"No, I, I . . ." Neal stammered. He brushed at the front of his wrinkled shirt, his head throbbing again. Unable to think clearly, he mumbled an apology for being late.

"Sorry—?" Danberg almost choked. Looking furious, he shuffled through a short stack of papers on his desk, finally finding a letter. He held it up in a beefy hand and said, "This is for you from the postmaster . . . a letter of warning."

Neal's stomach turned, the pain in his head making dots dance before his eyes. Jesus, he *was* sick. He reached for the letter, but the supervisor jerked it back out of reach.

Face growing even redder, Danberg said, "Uh-uh, you're late enough as it is. Go on to your case. I'll see you later." Still holding the letter, he turned back to the assignment board to study the various route numbers and assigned carrier names.

Too sick to argue, Neal stumbled away from Danberg's desk, moving along the row of blue carriers' cases, stopping at his route: City-21. Jesus, I should've said something to the big asshole, he thought, feeling angry and humiliated—

"Hey, Mac-the-gun," Ray Lewis said, backing out of his case, City-20. The tall black man was an old friend. They'd played city league basketball together for years, Neal firing up the outside bombs, Ray doing the rebounding and inside work. But that had been last year, before the accident.

"Better get hot, man," Ray suggested good-naturedly, gesturing at Neal's case, "there's a shitpot o' mail. . . . Say, you okay, Mac?" The smile disappeared from Ray's face. "You look kinda frayed around the edges."

Neal forced a grin. "I'm fine, Ray, fine . . . Just a late start, skipped breakfast, you know?"

Ray nodded. "Yeah, I dig." He patted Neal's shoulder and moved back in his case. "Well, hang in there, man, hang in. . . . "

Nodding to himself, Neal stepped into his own case. In front of him the six rows of numbered slots for letter-sized mail swam before his eyes, the color-coded streets blurring into a kaleidoscopic whirl—five hundred and fifty different addresses, arranged in the order of delivery. Eleven miles of walking to deliver it. Neal shook his head, feeling weary. He couldn't do it, not this morning, not today . . . but he knew he had no choice. Danberg and the letter. Danberg, the prick. A rush of anger partially revived Neal, but he couldn't risk anymore time off, sick or whatever. That's probably what the letter of warning was about, he guessed, glancing down at the mail lined up on his desk ledge—four feet of letters. Too many years invested. Jesus, he sighed, looking left at his flat case, full of magazines and other flats thrown the day before. To his right, the back of Ray's flat case. His stomach muscles knotted as he fought off the feeling of claustrophobia in the tiny cubicle. I am trapped, he thought, closing his eyes. *Kay in the doorway, smiling, beckoning*, so real, so near. . . . Neal blinked and focused on the tiny case numbers.

Biting down on his lower lip, Neal repeated Ray's advice: Hang in there, hang in there. He picked up a handful of mail and slowly began to throw letters into the case . . . 295 S. Hartson . . . Jay's Drugs . . . 104 S. Seymour . . ." Wait a minute," he murmured to himself, noticing the name on the letter: Johansen . . . Yeah, that's a forward, he reminded himself, placing the letter aside to be sent to the forwarding computer in Oakland. As he continued to work he felt himself slipping into the old familiar rhythm of it, throwing the letters into their proper slots, placing the forwards aside . . . bip, bip, bip, plunk, bip—

Suddenly, Neal stopped casing, staring at an address on a small letter: Resident, 300 S. Montgomery. No such number. South Montgomery didn't even have a 300 block, he thought. He tapped the letter on the case between 298 and 402 S. Montgomery, where the missing 300 should've been. It wasn't uncommon to get a bad number, but it was strange to get mail for a non-existent block. Maybe they meant 300 S. Hartson or 300 S. Seymour. Whatever, Neal thought, scribbling, *No Such Number, C-21*, on the letter. Then he set it aside to take to the throwback case later. But something about the piece of mail destroyed his rhythm, stirring a vague feeling of apprehension. He rested for a moment, closing his eyes. *The door, the number in the dream. . . .* He blinked, wondering what, if anything, it all meant. Maybe it's just the booze, he thought. I'm going around the bend. He shook his head, feeling sheepish.

At 11:10, Neal was the last carrier to tie out his route. Danberg had been by three times, grumbling under his breath. And finally, after pushing the tub of mail and parcels out back, Neal loaded his jeep and left the post office. He decided to stop for lunch before starting his route.

At the Circle K near South Seymour, Neal parked his jeep. He ate a ham sandwich and drank two beers. By noon the headache had almost disappeared and his stomach was settled.

He climbed back in the jeep and delivered the first of his route—parking and looping South Seymour and South Hartson; then he moved the vehicle to 102 South Montgomery for the next relay. After loading the flats and two bundles of mail into his carrying bag, Neal checked the back of the jeep for parcels: nothing for South Montgomery. He slipped the rubber band from the first bundle of letters and began working his way up the street: thumb through the mail, check for flats, drop it off, go to the next house—another rhythmic cycle. His mind drifted to Kay, the dream, the number on the door . . . and today's letter. At the end of the second block, he cut the lawn at 298—

Neal stopped suddenly, as if he'd run into an invisible wall. Silver was out, the big German Shepherd lying on the porch. "Easy, boy, easy," he whispered, backing away carefully from the huge dog. The Shepherd stood up, silver hair bristling along its neck, its black eyes watching Neal: then it growled—a dry rasp from deep in its throat, barely audible but full of menace—and began slowly creeping down the stairs, its eyes unwavering.

"Jesus," Neal swore, reaching for the can of dog spray at his side. "Easy, boy," he repeated in a hoarse voice, shaking the small can. "That's a good boy," he added, moving his carrying bag in front of himself like a shield.

The dog hesitated for a moment, watching Neal shake the can; then it dropped into a crouch—

"Silver," Mrs. Jones shouted, banging open the front screen door, "get in here!" Almost instantly the big dog turned and ran up the steps, disappearing into the house. "Sorry," the elderly woman said, wiping her hands on a red-checked apron. "I was making strawberry jam and forgot he was out. But Silver won't bite." She moved down the steps. "Got anything for here?"

Neal nodded, his legs rubbery. He handed the woman a letter and a *Sunset*. She took the mail, thanked him, and followed the dog back through the screen door. Neal swallowed hard, glued to the spot. He knew he was typical of most carriers, leary of all dogs, scared shitless of the big ones. Mrs. Jones was typical: *her* dog wouldn't bite. Yet 28,000 carriers a year were bitten.

After a few moments Neal moved stiffly to the corner of S. Montgomery and Spruce—a busy intersection. Still shaken by the confrontation with Silver, he stood at the curb for a minute, idly watching the cars blow by. The dull headache had returned. He closed his eyes, taking a deep breath. . . . He snapped his eyes open as a Kawasaki roared by. Stepping off the curb, Neal smiled. If there had been a 300 S. Montgomery, it would be here, in the middle of Spruce. He crossed the street and thumbed through the mail for 402 S. Montgomery. But he couldn't shake the lingering sense of unease stirred by the image of the door in the dream and the association with the bum piece of mail. His head throbbed.

As usual after work, Neal stopped at Jack's Club. After three double vodkas he felt much better. In the cool darkness the tension eased from his body as he listened to the jukebox, recognizing the twangy, old-man voice of John Connelly. The music helped; his headache was gone.

Suddenly light reflected in the mirror over the bar. Neal looked up and saw a woman framed in the doorway: long, dark hair, high cheekbones, a full smile. . . . "Jesus!" he gasped to himself, setting down his drink. He stared unbelieving. Then others crowded in behind the woman, and Neal realized she was too young, too short. But for a minute there. . . . He sighed deeply, and, with a trembling hand, picked up the glass and drained it. He signaled Jack for a refill, staring at himself in the mirror. Jesus, boy, you look like hell, he told himself, his gaze dropping to the crumpled uniform shirt. He tried to smooth out the wrinkles with his hand, remembering how neat Kay had been about his clothes—a fresh shirt to work each day. His face felt warm and he swallowed trying to clear the lump in his throat. Ignoring the fresh drink, Neal tossed a couple of bills on the bar, deciding to go home and do some laundry.

At the corner near his apartment Neal stopped at the 7-11. He picked up a box of detergent, a can of chili, some tortilla chips and a twelve-pack of Bud. Then he drove around behind the apartment to his stall. Before he could get out he heard someone shouting his name. "Mac, Mac . . . hi, Mac!"

It was his friend Billy, riding up on his Big Wheel.

"Hey, what do you say, pal?" Neal asked, stumbling as he climbed out of the car. He set the bag of groceries down on the dented hood of the Pinto, realizing he was beginning to feel the drinks.

"Hi . . . Mac," the five-year-old repeated breathlessly. "Guess what?"

Neal raised his eyebrows and shrugged, almost laughing at the boy's excitement. "Don't know."

"B'n W had kittens in the laundry room this morning, right in Mrs. Sem'ar's basket!"

Neal laughed, picturing the apartment busybody's face. Then he asked, "B'n W?"

The boy nodded. "You know, Jackie's cat."

"Oh, yeah," Neal said, controlling his glee. "I bet Mrs. Seminara was . . . surprised."

Billy frowned. "She got mad, told Jackie's mom, but—" the frown dissolved into a smile "—Jackie says I can have a kitty when they're bigger."

"That's great, let's celebrate." Neal pulled out the bag of tortilla chips and offered some to Billy, remembering the first time he'd seen the boy, about a year ago. Billy was riding his Big Wheel that time, too, around noon on a Sunday, wearing a pajama top but no bottom, crap running down his leg, his big eyes bright and shiny, even though he'd eaten nothing since dinner the night before. Neal had taken him upstairs to Kay. They'd cleaned the boy up, fed him and played with him for an hour or so until his mother, Sandy, had got up and come looking for her son. Kay had loved kids, but they never had any. Neal rubbed his numb face, closed his eyes. . . .

"Hey Mac, can I have some more?" The boy was tugging at Neal's pants' pocket.

"Well, I think it's dinner time, pal," Neal answered, roughing up the boy's hair.

Billy shrugged, then his face brightened. "Time for Sesame!"

Neal hoisted the boy up on his shoulders, then picked up the bag of groceries. "You'll be carrying me soon, bub."

Billy giggled, bouncing up and down as Neal climbed the apartment steps. Stumbling, Neal realized he was slightly drunk. At Billy's door he dropped the grocery bag, set the boy down, and rapped twice.

Sandy answered. "Hi, Mac."

Billy scooted past his mother headed for the TV set.

"Figured it was about dinner time for the boy," Neal said slowly, carefully keeping the slur from his voice. He bent over and picked up the grocery bag.

Sandy nodded. "Swanson's macaroni and cheese."

Neal shifted the bag. "Guess you had some excitement in the laundry room today?"

"Yeah," Sandy answered, chuckling, "freaked out old lady Seminara."

They laughed together, but then stood quietly, the silence growing awkward.

Finally: "Be nice for Billy," Sandy said, "the kitten, I mean."

"Yeah, pets are good for kids," Neal agreed, his face feeling stiff, his tongue thick. "Well, I better go."

Before he could move Sandy reached out and brushed his arm: a soft, intimate caress. "Thanks, Mac, for being so good to Billy. . . ."

He nodded.

"Maybe, we could get together, sometime . . . you know?"

Neal knew; and he was tempted. Sandy was kind of pretty, especially her braided hair—Irish Setter auburn—and her eyes, faded denim. Almost the exact color of. . . . He looked away, afraid to blink. "Yeah, maybe sometime," he whispered. He shifted the grocery bag again. "Well, I've got to do some laundry now." He didn't even try to hide the slur in his voice.

They stood silent for another moment, then she smiled. "Yeah, and I've got to put on the oven. See you, Mac."

For a few seconds he stood staring at her door, at the rusty number four hanging upside-down. Then he turned slowly and climbed the stairs, feeling a hundred years old.

Later that night, after the laundry, a plate of warm chili and half a dozen beers, Neal sat in his shorts staring at an old movie on the TV, *Treasure of the Sierra Madre*. It had had a cult following when Neal was going to junior college. The sound was turned down, and Neal stared at the flickering images, brooding: Kay . . . the dream . . . the door and number 300 . . . and the letter for 300 S. Montgomery. Something strange here, he thought, then he sat upright, remembering another cult at college. Kay had them over to the apartment once. A religous group —? Something about numerology. Damn, he couldn't remember, it'd all been mumbo-jumbo to him. But Kay had believed it. Was she trying to reach out to him? And why 300—? He rubbed his eyes, his head buzzing from the beer. Nah. He forced the crazy crap from his head, focusing back on the TV. The movie was drawing to a close, Bogart leading the mules toward the Mexican village. Neal drained another Bud, dropping the empty beer can onto the pile of crumpled empties beside his chair. His face felt numb, like after a visit to the dentist. He blinked, mouthing Bedoya's line to Bogart, *Hey, doan I know you?*. Unsteadily, Neal rose and moved close to the little screen. The bandits were slicing open the sacks of gold, letting the coarse dust trickle out and swirl away in the desert wind—

Neal snapped off the TV before the dumb anticlimax.

That night Neal had the dream again.

The next morning Neal was hungover again, his hands so shaky he couldn't shave, even after drinking a can of Bud. In the kitchen he held his breath and, with two hands holding the glass, drank a generous slug of vodka. The raw liquor burned his throat and made him retch, but he kept it down. In a few minutes a warmness spread from his stomach into his arms and legs, calming the tremor in his hands.

Later, after Neal had punched in, Danberg signaled for him to stop at the supervisor's desk. Then the big man announced loudly in his shrill voice, "The postmaster got a call from Mrs. Gary on South Hartson." Neal winced; the Garys lived at 102 and were constant complainers. "Well," Danberg continued, glancing at a note, "she says you did not pick up her outgoing mail yesterday—" He held up a beefy hand, interrupting Neal's explanation. "—I called her yesterday afternoon, and I explained that a carrier was not obligated to pick up outgoing mail when he had nothing to deliver, but she said you regularly leave *outgoing*, even after dropping off mail. She says it's a feud with you since she called in last December. Now McCarthy, we're a service organization. . . ." Danberg's face was squeezed up into a super-serious expression, as though he were lecturing a dull boy about life and death. ". . . and a carrier is a service person. If we don't provide service, we're out of business. We'll all be on the beach permanent. . . . "

Of course it was all bullshit, the lecture about service—management really cared only about production, loading the carriers down with circulars everyday—and the complaint. Neal felt the anger tightening his throat. Mrs. Gary enjoyed taking one mistake and making it an everyday occurrence. She could point the finger, somehow making her feel superior or something. Dammit. Neal swore silently; he'd made a real effort, even picking up letters when she had no mail, at least when he wasn't sick. The bitch. He felt dizzy, his legs weak. . . .

Danberg was standing silent, staring at Neal, waiting. Finally Neal sighed and nodded as if he'd listened to the whole lecture and understood. Danberg waved him away.

In front of his case Neal saw Ray Lewis shaking his head, an angry expression on his face. "Hey, man," Ray said, "don't pay that fool no mind. Everybody know he don't know dickshit."

They stepped into their individual cases, Ray still talking, but the angry tone dissolving. "You hear about Thompson?"

Neal picked up a handful of letters. "No."

"Well, he's pulling the plug next month."

Neal paused. Alvin Thompson retiring? He carried City-5 down at the First Street Branch office. Jesus . . . that meant City-5 would be up for bid—

"That's right," Ray said, as if reading Neal's mind. "And five's mostly driving, rural boxes and apartments with gang boxes. Only two short walking relays in Quail Trailer Park. No dogs. And best of all, you can kiss your buddy Danberg bye bye."

Neal smiled through his headache. Ray knew he wanted off City-21. Maybe he would bid Thompson's route. He probably had enough seniority to get it—

"Hey, Mac, you get five, you'll need a one-sleeved raincoat," Ray said, chuckling.

Neal shook his head at the old post office joke: on a jeep route, all that ever got wet during bad weather was one arm.

"Say, what about the fog?" Ray added. "Weird, eh? Like the stuff in them English horror flicks. Streets'll be slicker than old Gaylord's sinker."

"Yeah," Neal agreed, recalling Ray's outrage when the Giants traded away Gaylord Perry, the infamous spitball pitcher. . . . Unusual spring weather. Sometime during the night the fog had eased over the coastal mountains, filling the valley—

Neal stopped casing, staring at the address of a letter: Resident, 300 S. Montgomery. At first he thought it was another piece of mail: but no, it was the same piece from yesterday. There was his notation in the corner: *no such number, City-21.* He turned the letter over and picked up a slight scent. Familiar. He hadn't noticed it yesterday. He held the letter close and sniffed. . . . Jesus! Her scent? . . . And why had the clerks thrown it back? On impulse, Neal flipped the letter into the right side of 298 S. Montgomery's slot—where the missing 300 block should be. He knew it was silly. Yet after he put the letter up, he felt a sense of relief, like he had done the right thing. He left it in the case.

After delivering South Hartson, Neal rested for a minute at his jeep. He felt weak and a little sick. He rubbed his face and looked around. The fog had almost burned off, but the streets remained wet and slippery.

Neal got back in his jeep and eased it over to the low end of South Montgomery.

Putting the relay in his carrying bag, he thought again about Alvin Thompson's route—probably wasn't a mile of walking. And Danberg. Yeah, his mind was made up—a change would be good. Maybe he could ease up on the booze, let go of Kay. With a grunt, he hoisted the bag onto his shoulder, then began working the street. As he moved up the two hundred block, the mist seemed to thicken. Then Neal slowed his pace, remembering the confrontation with Silver the day before. He thumbed the mail and sighed with relief: nothing for 298—he wouldn't have to stop at the Jones's. Maybe he could use the fog as cover and slip by, even if the damn dog was out. He kept off the sidewalk, tiptoeing across the Jones's lawn, peering left, watching for the dog, his throat dry, his heart thumping against his ribs—

A sound raised the hair on the back of Neal's neck. A metallic jingle—? He wasn't sure. He stopped, cocked his head and listened. There, faint but discernible, the jingle of a dog collar. He swallowed, trying to work up moisture in his dry mouth. He squeezed the can of dog spray at his side, trying to draw some comfort from the tiny pseudo-weapon. Sweat trickled down his ribs. Several seconds ticked by, but nothing appeared. . . . Maybe he'd imagined the jingle, Neal told himself, or maybe it wasn't Silver after all. Still, he remained rooted in place, half expecting something to materialize in the fog, but there was only silence, grating silence. Where was that damn dog? Finally, listening intently, Neal forced himself to move on to the corner of Spruce.

For a moment he just stood on the curb, trying to relax. He'd been so tense his stomach muscles ached. He waited, letting his pulse slow. But there *was* something else. . . . His gaze was drawn to the top letter on his mail bundle: *Resident, 300 S. Montgomery.* He'd forgotten about the letter—his vision blurred and he felt dizzy. The fog swirled, thickening about him. He was standing in his own dream.

The mist seems so soft, protective. . . . Gradually his stiffness eases and he moves smoothly a few steps—Suddenly, far ahead in the mist, a rectangle of light. . . . A doorway, framing a woman, her face focused clearly in a beam of silvery light. . . . He moves toward the doorway and woman—A deep-throated half-cough, half-growl. A distant sound . . . chilling. Again . . . somewhere to the left of the doorway, an unnatural sound. Then, something large and heavy moving swiftly toward him. The raspy cough-growl again, this time louder, nearer. Run! Toward the doorway, Kay's outstretched hand. . . . Faster, faster. But there, cutting in front of him. . . . A shadow, features blurred. . . . A huge head and bared fangs, shiny eyes glowing like banked coals . . . and the creature is closing in, blocking him from Kay. No, no. Something snaps in his head, then a tingling as a feeling of tremendous power spreads out from his chest, down his arms to his fingertips; and a sound stirs deep in his throat, welling up, bursting from his lips—a cry that slashes the stillness; then rage, murderous rage overwhelming him. . . . He bends low and pounces on the creature, the thing twisting and struggling furiously to escape. But he locks his grip, and squeezes, crushes, until the thing goes limp. He raises it overhead and slams it down with tremendous force. . . . His heart pounding now, lungs gasping; he moans—

A high-pitched squeeling and two fuzzy orbs dancing into him . . . blackness. . . .

Dimly, Neal sees three people bending over him . . . strangers, their voices faint, distant. . . .

"My God, he's breathing. Call an ambulance!"

Footsteps, running, fading . . .

"Did you see him in the middle of the street. . . . I couldn't stop."

"He's a postman—"

"I couldn't stop."

"Good God, look what he did to that Shepherd."

"What's he grasping?"

"A letter . . ."

Neal tries to signal to them with his eyes . . . the letter, and who it was from . . . and he wasn't in the middle of Spruce. . . . No. They fade, blurring in the mist. Above the strangers, he sees an open doorway.

TEMPE

by

F.N. WRIGHT

Robert called one Thursday night and asked me to do him a small favor. You have to be careful in situations like this. Good friends can do-me-a-favor you to death; and it's the small ones that will kill you.

"Depends," I grumbled half-heartedly, "on what you want me to do."

"I sold my Z and I want you to deliver it to Palm Springs for me. It has to be there by Sunday afternoon."

"Why can't you do it?"

"I have business to attend to in San Francisco."

"Jesus, Robert. I don't think I can. I'm pretty busy myself these days."

"Dammit, Sam. You don't even have a job. How can you be busy?"

"I'm waiting for a phone call," I lied, "I might have something lined up."

"Bullshit. You're lying to me." Robert knew I avoided work with the determination of a spinster defending her maidenhead.

"So, what's new?" I said. "I don't want to go to Palm Springs."

"Not even as a favor to me?"

"Not even as a favor to you."

"I'll pay all of your expenses and give you $25 for your time and trouble."

"Make it $50 and —"

"Okay. $50."

"I'll consider it," I continued.

"Dammit, Sam. *Please*."

"Fifty and all expenses?"

"Yes."

"Make it a hundred and I'll do it."

"A hundred?"

"That's what I said."

"Okay, you Goddam extortionist," he laughed, "I'll bring the car by Saturday."

"Don't forget the hundred."

I hung up the phone and raced my bladder to the bathroom. I won, but not by much. After shaking it more than the prescribed three times, I went into the kitchen for a beer.

Six or seven beers later, I remembered that I hadn't seen my grandmother for 9 or 10 years. I picked up the phone and called Robert.

"Yeah?" he mumbled, struggling from a sound sleep.

"Robert, I haven't seen my grandmother for 9 or 10 years."

"What?" He was half asleep.

"I want to see my grandmother."

"Jesus Christ, Sam. It's two a.m.!" He was wide awake now.

"Is it?" I asked innocently.

"What do you want? Don't tell me you've changed your mind."

"No. It isn't that. I want to visit my grandmother."

"Sam, have you been drinking?" I could tell by the tone of his voice that he was trying to be patient with me.

"No," I belched in his ear.

"Then why in the hell are you calling me at two in the morning to tell me you want to visit your fucking grandmother?" Robert's patience had run out.

"Robert, I'm ashamed of you," I slurred, "she's 83 if she's a day. She shouldn't be fucking at her age."

"Get to the point! What does your grandmother have to do with our agreement? What do you want from me *now*?"

Had I been sober I would've picked up on his what-do-you-want-from-me-now crap and told him to stick his Z and Palm Springs up someone's ass. He started this do-me-a-favor shit, not me. Unfortunately, I was not sober. "She lives in Tempe," I said.

"Arizona?"

"Yeah."

"Sam, you have me confused."

"I figure I might as well take advantage of the opportunity and visit her. I—"

"You mean take advantage of me, don't you?"

"If you bring the car by tomorrow," I said, ignoring his remark, "I can drive down during the evening and spend Saturday with her. If I leave Tempe that night or early Sunday morning, I'll still be able to get to Palm Springs as scheduled."

"Your grandmother," Robert chuckled, "come on, who's the female?"

"I'm telling the truth, Robert."

"Do you love your grandmother, Sam?"

"Beats the shit out of me. Like I said, I haven't seen the old broad for 9 or 10 years."

"Why do you want to visit her now?"

"I just remembered that she's old and rich. I want to remind her that she has a grandson."

"I'll bring the car tomorrow afternoon," Robert laughed, "just be sure to give her my love when you see her."

Robert brought the car by my apartment Friday afternoon. "One more thing," I said as he handed me the keys, a gasoline credit card and five twenties.

"What?"

"Better give me a couple of real credit cards."

"And why would I want to do something as stupid as that?"

"Food and motel expenses."

"You *are* going to Tempe to see a girlfriend, aren't you."

"No, Robert. I'm really going to visit my grandmother." He believed me this time because he thought I was sober.

"Take your personal expenses out of the hundred."

"That's drinking money."

"No," he said firmly, "no credit cards."

"Forget it," I said, dropping everything in his lap. Everything but the five twenties, which were already in my wallet.

"You borderline criminal," he grumbled, putting the car keys and gasoline credit card on the table beside his chair. "Don't screw up. Please have the car in Palm Springs Sunday before six." He put his Mastercharge and American Express cards on the table and left before I could hit him up for anything else.

I packed a suitcase, rolled a few joints and hit the road. After stopping at one of my favorite greasy spoons for a chili-cheeseburger, I rolled into a liquor store and picked up a couple of sixers of Schlitz.

The late Friday afternoon L.A. freeway traffic was, as usual, suicidal—packed bumper to bumper with poor, wrung-out-by-the-boss, 9-to-5 bastards with brains floating in happy-hour martinis hurrying home to frigid, gin-soaked, chocolate-fattened housewives, snivelling snot-nosed, ungrateful sons and spoiled daughters.

With Joe Schlitz, co-pilot, sitting on the seat beside me in a cooler packed with ice, I somehow managed to survive the swarm of assholes and their kamikaze driving tactics.

I arrived in Tempe a little after midnight. It was still early enough to find some action. My nose picked up the unmistakable odor of pussy and led me to a college campus.

There was one thing on my mind as I rented a room at a nearby Holy Idiot motel. As soon as I was checked in, I was going to go out and get me one of those young, educated pussies.

The motel manager was middle-aged and miserable. She looked like she had spent the past twenty years married to a Sunday afternoon football freak who never washed his feet.

"Any bars in the neighborhood?" I asked as I signed the register.

"Yeah," she grunted sullenly, "we have a bar."

"Is it a college hang-out? I'm looking for a little action."

"You look too old for the college kids, mister," she smirked, "and a little too rough around the edges to appeal to those young girls. Their pace would kill you."

It was obvious the old bitch wasn't going to direct me to a bar where I could chase some college stuff, which was okay with me. I was a good ol' California cowboy with a six-shooter in his pants. "What time do the streets roll up around here?" I asked.

"One a.m., mister," she said, handing me a receipt and walking away.

Shit, there wasn't enough time to put my nose to work. Not even enough time to put my things in my room if I wanted a couple of beers before going to bed. I decided to check out the motel bar. Maybe there would be something in there to chase. "Jesus, one fucking o'clock," I complained as I entered the Holy Idiot bar.

They called it the Glenn Miller Memorial Room. I could see why. There was a spry old chicken of 70 spinning swing records on a brand new, light-flashing disco machine. Bones creaked and groaned as ancient-legged bodies boogied to the sound booming from four huge speakers. The volume was cranked up full blast, and when I saw the assortment of hearing aids on the dance floor, I knew why.

I was getting a headache, so I ordered a double shot of tequila to go with my beer. I looked in the mirror behind the bar and watched the seniors behind me dance to "Chattanooga Choo-Choo." It was depressing.

I ordered another shot of tequila and watched the little hand on the clock creep towards one as the big hand crawled towards twelve.

After my third double shot of tequila and third or fourth beer, I began wondering if my grandmother was in the room. When there was a lull in the music I hollered, "Granny, are you here?"

No one heard me but the bartender, and he looked pissed. He walked over to me and said, "That wasn't funny, mister. Finish your beer and get out of here."

He looked like a punch-drunk boxer who'd taken one too many blows to the head. I figured I could take him out with one shot to his overhanging gut, but I didn't think I could handle the crowd of seniors if they attacked me with their canes for beating up their bartender. I drained my beer, stood up, spit on the carpet, and left.

Outside there were two young punks trying to break into the Z. "Hey!" I yelled. "What in the fuck do you think you're doing?"

They looked up, saw me coming at them and took off running. They ran around to the side of the motel and entered an unlocked door that led to the kitchen. It was closed for the evening and pitch black. By the time I found the light switch they had escaped through another door on the other side of the room. I turned off the light and went back outside.

The motel manager and two cops were there to greet me. She was agitated and the two cops were nervously toying with their holstered guns. Their trigger fingers looked extremely itchy.

"See, I told you I heard noises in the kitchen," the bitch spat triumphantly.

The two cops stood there grinning at me as they continued playing with their still-holstered guns. "What were you doing in the kitchen, boy?" the one with crooked, yellow teeth finally asked me.

"Yeah, what were you doing in the kitchen, boy?" his pimply-faced partner echoed.

I was a good ten years older than either one of them and they were calling *me* boy. Two young, wet-behind-the-ears hoodlums with G.E.D. certificates. The only difference between them and the punks who'd been trying to break into the Z was their uniforms. Hell, that made them twice as dangerous, and me more nervous than they were. I wasn't about to do anything to give them an excuse to pull out those small cannons they were carrying. These two faggots would've been dangerous with BB guns.

"I caught two punks trying to break into my car," I said. "I chased them into the kitchen. I lost them, but if you hurry you — "

"I want him out of here," the manager screeched, "he's already caused trouble in the bar!"

The cops' eyes lit up like pinball machines. "What kind of trouble, Madge?" Crooked Teeth asked.

"Nothing serious. I just want him out of his room."

"Hear that, boy?" Crooked Teeth chuckled, "she wants you to vacate the premises."

I wasn't about to argue with three maniacs—especially when two of them were uniformed juvenile delinquents. "Okay," I agreed, "I'll get a room somewhere else, but I want my thirty dollars back."

The two juveniles looked at Madge. She shook her head no. "See that, boy," Crooked Teeth said, "Madge says no."

"Look, officers," I protested, "I haven't even been in that room. I want a refund."

"He didn't even pay cash," Madge complained bitterly.

"You trying to pull a scam, boy?" Crooked Teeth growled.

"I'm not asking for a cash refund. She can tear up the charge slip and I'll be on my — "

"I'm all booked up now," Madge grumbled. "I could've rented that room an hour ago. Now it's too late. He gets nothing."

"Want to make something out of it?" Pimple-face begged.

"No, I'll go," I said, figuring Robert could take care of the problem when I got back to Los Angeles. It was his credit card and he was a damn good lawyer.

Crooked Teeth and Pimples escorted me to the Z. As I was getting in, Crooked Teeth asked me if I'd been drinking. "Yeah, I've had a couple," I replied.

"Then I wouldn't drive anywhere if I were you," Pimples cautioned.

"And if you stay here we'll bust you for loitering," Crooked Teeth said.

"Fuck both of you," I muttered under my breath as I started up the Z and pulled out of the parking lot.

They got into their squad car and tail-gated me for several blocks, blinding me with their brights shining in the Z's rear view mirror. It was irritating.

I finally pulled over to the side of the road to see what the hell was going on. Crooked Teeth turned on the flashing red lights and pulled in behind me. I got out of the Z and waited for them.

"We think you're driving under the influence." Crooked Teeth smirked.

"You have been driving erratically," Pimples said.

"You assholes have been blinding me with your brights and tail-gating my ass," I said as my anger finally surfaced. They reached for their guns and I shut up.

First they relieved me of my driver's license. Then Crooked Teeth put me through a series of sobriety tests while Pimples radioed to see if I had any outstanding warrants. They were both disappointed when I passed the tests and the dispatcher informed them that I was a good citizen—or at least not wanted anywhere. "What are we going to do with him?" Pimples asked.

"I guess we'll have to let him go," Crooked Teeth replied reluctantly.

"Why don't we take him to headquarters and give him a breathalyzer?" Pimples slyly suggested.

Crooked Teeth's yellow smile lit up his face as he reached for his cuffs. "We're taking you in, boy," he hissed, "turn around." He made damn sure the cuffs were sadistically tight. Then he put me in the squad car while Pimples locked up the Z.

As we neared the station, I leaned forward and said, "I've got your asses, fuck-heads. You neglected to read me my rights."

Pimples turned angrily in his seat and glared through the protective screen. He was snarling mad and his mouth curled into a sneer as he launched a verbal assault. "Listen, punk," he snarled, "you want us to pull over and —" My words located the small target his brain offered and torpedoed his attack in mid-sentence. A worried droop replaced the sneer on his face. He looked over at Crooked Teeth and mumbled, "Do you think we fucked up?"

Crooked Teeth hesitated a moment then smirked. "Nah. It's his word against ours."

"Right!" Pimples relaxed. "Hear that, boy?" he said as his confidence returned. "It's your word against ours. You don't have a snowball's chance in hell."

They took the cuffs off when we reached the station and shoved a form in my face. "Sign it," Crooked Teeth commanded. I began reading.

"Sign it, boy," Pimples echoed.

"If you don't mind, I'll read it first."

"Put down," Crooked Teeth said, "that he refused to sign — "

"I didn't say I wouldn't sign the sonofabitch," I protested, "but I don't sign anything without reading it first."

Pimples looked at Crooked Teeth with question marks for eyes as I rapidly scanned the document. It gave them permission to give me a breathalyzer test. "You heard me," Crooked Teeth said, "he ref — "

"I'll sign the sonofabitch," I said, "give me a fucking pen."

"Now we're going to give you a breathalyzer, smartass," Crooked Teeth said as I handed him the signed form.

"What reading makes me legally drunk in the state of Arizona?" I asked.

"Put down that he refused to take the test," Crooked Teeth said, "the sonofabitch'll lose his license for six months."

I blew them a balloon the size of a basketball before Pimples could put anything down. I passed it to Crooked Teeth, sorry it wasn't a fucking medicine ball.

"1.0%!" Crooked Teeth exclaimed when the results were read, "throw his ass in the drunk tank."

I'd made it. I was legally drunk as far as the state of Arizona was concerned. "Where's my cap and gown?" I asked as they led me to the drunk tank.

"You won't be such a smartass after the judge gets your ass in the morning," Crooked Teeth chuckled.

"He'll throw the book at you," Pimples chortled as they locked the door behind me.

It was like any other drunk tank I'd ever been in, but this one was even colder than usual. It was like being locked up in a cold storage locker. My balls crawled up and huddled in my belly, seeking warmth from the cold. It was no use. There was a large vent in the ceiling blowing out gusts of air at gale force.

I walked over and banged on the solid steel door. Nothing happened. I banged on it again, longer and louder. It swung open with a clang. A huge cop scowled at me. A huge, warm cop. "Whaddya want, punk?" he growled.

"It's cold in here. Can you turn that off?" I gestured towards the vent.

"Get over in the corner," he said, pointing towards the urine trough, "and sit down!"

"Goddamnit, its co—" He slammed the door in my face, I might have been from California, but I didn't have to put up with this shit. I was still a citizen, sober or not, of the United States of America. La-de-fucking-da. I banged on the door again.

A Chicano cop opened it this time. I smiled at him. He'd been through enough prejudice and shit in his life to relate to my predicament. He showed me his white teeth and said, "What do you want, man?"

"It's cold in here. Think you could turn tha—"

"Look, man," he said, grabbing my shirt, "you were told to sit down over in that corner."

I knocked his hands away and stepped back. "I'm not trying to cause any trouble, motherfucker," I hissed, "but you don't have any right to abuse me. Pull another number like that and I'll shove that badge up your ass."

"Hank!" he hollered. The huge warm cop lumbered into the tank. "He's giving me trouble, Hank."

"No trouble, Hank," I said, "I'll go sit in the corner like a good boy." It was too late. I'd lost my temper like an idiot. I'd finally given them what they'd all been waiting for, a chance to prove to themselves what big, he-men, macho cops they thought they were.

I tried to ease over to the corner, but Hank worked in behind me. He put me away with a choke-hold while his Chicano compatriot took a couple of cheap shots at my gut.

I woke up a few hours later, rolled over, and vomitted in the urine trough. There was a new shift of Tempe's finest on duty. One of them brought me in a tray of food. "Have a nice nap?" he smirked.

I tried to tell him to fuck off, but my voice was gone. Hank's choke-hold had wounded my vocal chords.

"Enjoy your breakfast," he said, spitting on the food, "the judge'll be here in an hour or so."

I dumped the food in the trough, then went over and sat down next to the door. It finally opened three hours later and I was taken upstairs to see the judge.

He was young, supposedly one of the youngest judges in the country. He had peach fuzz on his cheeks and a cherry in his pants. Corruption hadn't filled his wallet. Yet. That would come with time and the favors he would owe others to keep his position. Yeah, the bastards would get to him sooner or later. They always did.

The charges were read. Hoarse voice and all, I gave it my best shot. INNOCENT. That's how I pleaded to all charges.

"Where are the arresting officers?" the judge asked. Silence. "Well, where are they?" More silence.

"Your honor," I rasped, "I have a few complaints to make."

"What?" He hadn't been able to understand me.

"I have — "

"Seabolt. Samuel Seabolt," he muttered, looking more closely at my file, "Are you related to Francine Seabolt?"

I nodded my head yes and rasped, "She's my grandmother."

"Recess!" Peach fuzz called out. Jesus, it was like being in kindergarten again. He took me back to his chambers and poured me a drink.

I tossed it down and held out my glass for a refill.

"She's a good woman," he said, refilling my glass and pouring himself a drink. "She helped put me through law school." He raised his glass, "For Granny Franny." We drank to the old broad and the judge refilled our glasses.

The whiskey helped ease the pain in my throat. It was still only a hoarse whisper, but my voice was gaining a little strength. "Judge," I said, "I want to — "

"You don't have to say anything," he interrupted, "I'm dismissing all the charges against you."

"Because of granny?"

He frowned and said, "I don't operate like that."

"Sorry," I said.

"Believe it or not, there are some decent men on Tempe's police force." I didn't believe it. "One of them made it a point to meet with me this morning. He told me what you experienced while in custody. I want you to give me a written statement."

"Why?"

"Sooner or later, with this kind of evidence, we'll be able to weed out the bad officers on the force."

I didn't have the heart to burst his idealistic bubble, so I gave him a written statement. We shook hands. Then he gave me his card and told me to call him if I had any more trouble.

I went downstairs and asked the dispatcher where my car was

impounded. She was a fox with a body her uniform couldn't hide. This was one cop I could have learned to like in a minute. She showed me a lot of white teeth and sent me to a lot on the other side of town. The Z wasn't there.

I called from a pay phone and told her there seemed to be some kind of mix-up. "Gee, I'm sorry, sir," she said with sincerity, "I made a mistake. It's at lot #105."

She gave me the address and I grabbed another cab, spending ten dollars to get there. The Z wasn't there either. I called the judge and told him I was getting the royal runaround.

"I'll take care of it," he replied tersely. "Where are you?" I told him where I was. "Someone will bring you your car," he promised.

"Do me a favor, Judge," I said, "the dispatcher is the one who's been giving me the runaround. Think maybe you could get her relieved and send her with the car?"

He chuckled and said he would see what he could do.

She showed up with the Z an hour later. There was a wise-assed grin plastered to her face. "Sorry, sir," she said, getting out of the car. She showed a lot of nice leg in the process, but I was too pissed to enjoy it.

I got in as she walked around to the passenger side. "Call a cab, bitch," I said, pulling away before she could get in.

It was 8 p.m. by the time I found granny's house, a castle-sized mansion that occupied the best of two blocks. I figured it was probably past her bedtime, but I wasn't about to leave town without seeing her. Not after what I'd been through. Afterall, I didn't want her to forget that she had a grandson. Especially with that young judge around. I didn't want him to get my share of the inheritance.

I lifted the heavy brass knocker and hammered loudly so she'd be sure to hear me, asleep or not.

"Easy out there," a woman's voice called out with strength, "I'm not deaf."

"Sorry," I said sheepishly, realizing I was still hammering away.

She stopped on the other side of the door and asked, "Who is it?"

"Grandma Seabolt?"

"Is that you, Judge? Little Jerry?"

"No. It's me. Sammy."

"Sammy? Sammy, my grandson?"

"Yes."

"The one I haven't seen in ages?"

"That's the one."

The heavy oak door swung open and granny reached out and grabbed my arm. "Get your ass in here and drink a beer with your grandmother," she said, giggling like a young schoolgirl.

Granny was small, but solid. She didn't look a day over 50. Her eyes were bright and her walk sure and steady. Nothing at all what I expected. She had the spunk of a young filly. "What's the matter," she asked, handing me a cold beer, "cat got your tongue?"

"Are you sure you're 83?"

"87," she replied, taking a drink of beer, "Always drink beer right from the bottle, Sammy. It tastes much better that way."

Granny and I drank beer and bullshitted for several hours. At one point in the conversation, I asked her if she ever hung out at the Holy Idiot bar. "Which one?" she asked, handing me another beer.

"The one with the Glenn Miller Memorial Room."

"You have to be kidding. With them fogeys? There isn't an old fart in the crowd who can keep up with your grandmother."

I believed that. Hell, I was having trouble keeping up with her, and I'm a beer drinker who usually sets the pace when drinking with friends. But granny was setting the pace this night.

I looked up at the clock hanging on the wall behind her. It was 11:45. "Granny," I said, "it's almost midnite. I'm not keeping you up, am I?"

"I'm just getting warmed up," she said, getting us another round.

We continued bullshitting and drinking beer. By the time two o'clock rolled around, I was behind a couple of beers and ready to pass out. Granny looked like she was going to last until dawn. I got up and took another piss. When I got back, the old broad took pity on my condition and put me to bed.

She was in my room with a steaming cup of black coffee at six a.m. sharp. "Here," she said, opening the curtains and letting the bright light of a new day pour into the room, "drink this. Breakfast will be ready in fifteen minutes."

My body somehow managed to survive the shock of sunlight and eggs sunnyside up. I was ready to hit the road by seven. Granny asked me if I had a cooler and I said yes. "Go get it and I'll pack you some cold beer for the road," she said.

A fit of depression settled over me as I watched Tempe disappear in the Z's rearview mirror. My throat hurt, I had a hangover, and I knew I was going to have to find a job when I got back to L.A. There was no way I was going to get an inheritance from Grandma Seabolt. I started laughing and pressed down on the accelerator pedal. I was doing 110 within seconds, still laughing as the tears streamed down my face.

THE KILLING OF TRAIN-MAN BROWN

by

WILL BEVIS

I was only 17 when I first met Walker Brown. Everybody called him "Train-Man Brown," or just "Train-Man." Not "Trainman"—that was too soft. The emphasis was always on "Man." Evidently Train-Man Brown had kicked a few butts in his lifetime and had earned quite of bit of respect along the way. It was assumed he was crazy—at least most people said he was. But I never believed it, and he became the best friend I ever had.

Our friendship started on my first day of working on what people called the gravy train. Believe me, it was no such thing. I remember the year, 1963, because Walker died only a year later, when the government sort of pulled the rug out from under him. Took away his reason to live.

I was green back then, naive as can be. The postmaster, Eulie Tatum, he had me come in that first morning at 9:00. He handed me a bulging 40 lb. mailbag and said, "It only takes Junior Berry 55 minutes to deliver this little shoestring walking route. Let's see how long it takes a young stud like you."

I could hear the other mailmen in the old post office snickering as I shouldered that first heavy bag. It had never crossed my mind that mail could be that heavy. Gravy train? Don't never believe it.

The other mailmen wouldn't let up with their comments—talking about how I might not be back today, or even tomorrow. And one of them yelled out that no matter HOW LONG it took to be damn sure that old Train-Man Brown got all his precious junk mail—or he'd be calling the postmaster to file a complaint. "Train-Man who?" I thought. I already had all the problems I needed.

26

I made my way past all the comedians heading for the door, when Junior Berry himself calls me aside and says, "Don't listen to them, Scooter. You just watch the street signs and the addresses on the houses and check the mail against them, and you'll do OK."

That made me feel better. I pushed through the heavy loading dock doors, thinking maybe I had found a friend in Junior Berry—even though he had called me Scooter out of the clear blue sky and thus given me a nickname I'd have to live with for as long as I carried the mail. I thought he had cared enough to give me that "advice"—not knowing he was laughing behind my back with the rest of them. I soon found out why.

It was because the first intersection I came to out the door *didn't have any street signs.* There weren't even any houses to have numbers on them for a whole block in any direction—except for one run down old shack across from where I stood.

I'd been had. Heck, I didn't know where I was at. I'd never even been to that little town before but once, and that was when I was a little kid and we'd come over to catch a train. There I was, standing on that corner—that heavy mailbag already rubbing my shoulder raw—while I looked up and down two almost deserted streets, not knowing which way to go. And damn me if it didn't look like rain. I felt like sitting down on the curb and crying—and then kicking that mailbag down in the gutter and quitting.

But help came, in the person of Train-Man Brown, bless him. He had been sitting on the porch of that old shack across the street, watching me struggle with myself and my predicament—and shaking his head. I hadn't even seen him—he was so black he was lost in the deep morning shadows of the porch.

He stood up slowly, and he was tall. That's what made me finally see him. He was a big man. Too big not to see. He came down the rotting wooden steps toward me saying "You're a new kid, ain't you?" moving as slowly and confidently as I ever saw anybody ever do anything.

"Yes, sir," I said, when he was face to face with me. He didn't ask for no "sirs" but I could tell right away he was the kind of man who deserved it. In his seventies, I guessed. I remember how sad his eyes were. He kind of smiled and said, "Don't worry, Sonny. We'll fix Eulie Tatum's wagon."

"We will?" I said, not knowing if I was about to go from worse to completely terrible.

Then he reaches over, takes a pen from MY pocket, reaches in MY mailbag, pulls out a certified letter, and starts drawing me a map right on the front of it.

I scratched my head. "I don't know why they do stupid stuff like this," he said. "Send you out so unprepared. That's why I never worked a day on the ground for them. They're different—or we are—and I never had no use for postmasters nor them for me. We always worked alone and did a damn good job of it, too—without a damned postmaster looking over our shoulders all the time—ready to jump on your head for the slightest mistake."

Man, I didn't know what on earth he was talking about. I was just glad he was helping me. Real help, too, not Junior Berry help. This black man—he didn't tell me who he was and I was in too much shock to ask—he drew a map, not just of the area, but of every turn and doubleback and fish-hook on the whole route I had to walk. He knew *everything* about it—even where the bad dogs were to look out for.

And the funniest thing: as he explained what he was drawing, he sort of *swayed back and forth* where he stood. I couldn't help but notice it— and I can still see him doing it in my mind, right now, back and forth, back and forth, as if he were on a ship on the ocean. I remember thinking he must have been a sailor back when he was young.

When he was through mapping he said, "You'll be all right now, Sonny—that is if they didn't shuffle the mail on you, and you don't slip up and drop it."

I didn't even know what "shuffling" was back then. Can you believe people would mix-up your mail behind your back just to make this "gravy train" harder for you than it naturally was? Well, buddy, they will. But they didn't do it to me that day. I guess they figured they wouldn't have to. I'd never make it anyway.

I thanked Walker for his help and started out—feeling a whole lot better—when he calls out to me: "Ain't I got no mail today, Sonny?"

I felt bad. I told him I was sorry—I had been so glad he'd helped me that I'd forgotten all about that he might get some mail just like somebody else. And get some mail he did. That day and every day. Huge bundles rubber-banded to keep them together. He got more junk mail than anybody else in town—than anybody else in the world, I'd be willing to bet—and one day I found out why.

But I want you to know I got back to the post office that first day in 57 minutes flat. Nobody else had even left on their routes yet. I swear, their mouths fell wide open when they saw me come through the double doors with an empty bag and a smile on my face. They had been so prepared to laugh their butts off when I came in late after dark—or even quit. They couldn't believe it. Neither could the postmaster.

He called me into his dinky office and said, "You had help, didn't you? Can't be no other way. You had to have had help."

I just said, "What?"

He said, "Train-Man Brown. It must have been him. He helped you, didn't he? He must have. He knows more about the mail than anybody else around here 'cept me."

I finally owned up to it. I said, "Well, a man helped me, but I don't know who he was."

"An old black man," Postmaster says to me. "Still got a barrel chest and tall—and got a manure load of bulk mail? And swayed where he stood—like he was standing on a moving train? Like this?"

Eulie Tatum swayed back and forth in front of me. It was a really poor imitation. Didn't have any rhythm to it at all. Train-Man had been smooth as butter spread back and forth on fresh bread.

"Yeh, Postmaster," I said. "That was him."

"That's Train-Man," he said, shaking his head. "Boy, you've got the job—but stay away from that Walker Brown."

I didn't ask him why. But I didn't stay away from Walker Brown, either. He became my good friend, and the only friend I had for quite a while.

He was a mail train man—or he had been. A real one. He was a special breed of disappearing old buffalo—an old postal clerk that had worked the mail on the trains, back when you had to know every town in every state in the entire union—not just a few zip codes—to do the job right.

It took a long time for him to open up to me. He didn't like regular mail clerks or city or rural carriers—or just about anybody, for some reason. But when he did break down and start talkin' to me, he opened up a whole new world I'd never even known existed: the world of the mail trains. A world that's gone now.

Walker's father had been a train man too. He'd often taken Walker along to Columbia and Raleigh, and even on up to Pittsburgh and beyond. Said his father told him, "Walker, ain't no racism in a moving mail train. It's men working together to get a job done and done right."

Walker's daddy had even been in the Great Trans-Continental Mail

Train Race of 1889, and he sure was proud of that—even though it was something I'd never heard of. But to hear Walker tell, it was a big affair back then, boy I tell you. About like a Superbowl or nuclear accident is today, I guess.

Walker knew everything about the mail trains, and Lord, I grew to love this old black man and all his stories and factualities. He could tell you, for example, which ones had been robbed, and how many times and by who—and whether they were caught and hung or not—with no exceptions.

And he could tell you how a letter or a postcard would have to train to get from here to anywhere in the old days—or even at that moment, for that matter. He'd rode a lot of trains in his lifetime—all of them at least once, he swore. And he'd thrown the mail in mailcars for over FIFTY years, before they'd made him clear out and retire.

I was surprised, but he really grew to trust me. I say surprised, 'cause one day he shared a big secret with me. Took me down in his basement not too awful long before he died. There was an old postage meter down there and a solid oak mail case—both off a forgotten old train wreck, he claimed. Well, it's illegal to have a government postage meter or other postal property, even old stuff. But Train-Man had it anyway, and he didn't misuse it or anything. You know, sending free mail or the like. Far as I know, there wasn't anybody he wanted to write to.

He just had it to remind him of what had been, of what he used to be and what he used to do. And there was something else down there in that basement. As a matter of fact, it was everywhere in the basement you looked. Junk mail. Lord God! Boxes and boxes and boxes and boxes of it.

What did he want it all for? Why, Walker would pick up a huge handful of that junk at random and start throwing it with his *left* hand into that oak mail case—reading the addresses backhanded off the envelopes and throwing that junk back to wherever in hell it had come from. He'd whiz it into the correct slot on that case at 5 or 6 or even 7 pieces a second—and buddy, that's FAST. Put any distribution clerk I ever have known since to shame, that's for sure. Each letter would hit the back of that oak case and tap like a jazz drummer beatin' out a fancy rhythm in quadruple time or something.

That's why he got all that junk mail: so he could *live* again. Come alive again. I remember him swaying down in that basement like he was on that train sorting the MUST-GO mail right that moment—the letters just a-flying out of his old bony fingers into the proper case holes like quicksilver—like the mail was just *flowing* through his hands to exactly where it should go.

He'd keep on throwing—even while he would glance at me, and smile and say something like, "Now, boy, this is the way we did it on THE TRAINS. FAST. You got to, 'cause you hook the mail at one town and you got to have it ALL worked and pouched 'for the next town a quarter of a mile away—cause the train DON'T STOP FOR NOBODY—not a mail train. Not even for Uncle Sam or Jefferson Davis."

Walker smiled all the time he was talking, or even thinking, about when he used to be a train man. But any other time, he was sad. He had hollowed eyes. Down at the mouth. And that was most of the time. I only saw him get angry once. He was telling me about the strikes the railroad unions used to have every now and then—and how it would shut down the mail trains. He got all hot thinking about it, that's for sure. I found out much later from the postmaster that Train-Man had punched out a conductor and TWO engineers during one strike and got in to serious trouble about it—even though they had started the mess. When Walker himself talked about it all he ever said was he had just wanted to get those trains moving—just wanted to ride that train and get that mail out all up and down the line—like it was supposed to be done. Clickey-clack, he would say, throw the mail—sleep in a strange town— and do it all over again the next day. The way he told it, it sounded like heaven.

You know, some people say that the Post Office killed the trains—and itself—when they switched to trucks and airplanes—that they started dying when they took the men and the mail off the trains.

Well, I don't know nothing about all that. It's beyond me. But I do know this: When they killed the mail trains, they killed Walker Brown. Before 1964 he still knew some people on the trains—even though he was long retired—and they'd let him ride some and throw the mail when they knew there wasn't no management on down the line. Supervisors didn't like that a bit. But in 1964 they stopped the mail trains. The powers that be did. I guess it was Congress, I don't know.. But I remember when it was, 'cause it wasn't more than three days after they took the mail off the trains for good that Walker Brown died. Just up and died. I guess he felt there was nothing for him to live for, if he couldn't at least ride and throw the mail even just every now and then. That era was gone, and I guess he just decided to go on with it.

He didn't have a wife to pull him through, I know that. He said she'd left him when they were both young 'cause he was always gone on the rails. Had kids though. I know 'cause they showed up out of nowhere and sold all his belongings at an auction held right in the front yard of his shack. It was horrible. Years later I saw that old postage meter at a sale barn. I know it was the same one 'cause I can still see Walker standing there at it, his back to me, throwing the mail. Nobody was bidding on it cause they didn't know what it was. It looked like junk. I wanted to buy it, but I had a wife and kids of my own by that time, and I wasn't thinking too much about Walker Brown then . . . like I do now.

There's a memory in my mind—clear as the crystal on a fine railroad watch. I'm a little boy standing on the platform of the Warner Robbins train station. The station keeper is standing there with my mother and me. He's got that hat on that only station keepers could wear. She's holding my hand. Suddenly I see a train ROARING down the track toward us at fifty miles an hour to nothing and I shout excitedly, "Mommy, LOOK—here comes our train!"

But the railroad man shakes his head as the train approaches and says, "No, young man. That's not your train—that's the 45 East—strictly a mail train. Nothing else. Got to be in Atlanta this afternoon sharp. Don't stop for God nor the devil."

I can see it now, just as if it was happening again. The huge, black locomotive barreling down the track—zooming by—smoking like a hotel on fire - not slowing down a hair. Then several cars back a hook snatches a canvas mail pouch like a New York thief grabbing a purse and being gone with it scot-free.

And there, standing in the mailcar doorway, is a smiling black man in the absolute prime of his life—one who looks so very happy with what he is doing and who he is. He takes the mail off the hook with ease—like it didn't weigh nothing at all, like it was the most precious stuff in the world—as his car passes right in front of me. He sees me and waves— and then takes that mail inside to work it, to make sure every man, woman and child in America gets every single letter he's responsible for—the first time, with no mistakes.

It's only a split-second memory, but I can see it like with a magnifying glass—and oh, how good it makes me feel. The man was a train man, and I keep thinking to myself it was Walker Brown, sure as the world. It had to be. There's no one else it could have been.

Anyway, that's the way I want to remember him. Smiling and

throwing the mail and riding the mail train as it click-clacks away, until it is silent—and disappears down the end of the long tracks.

I guess it's a good thing you went ahead and died, Walker, so you can't see what's going on. They won't even let a man throw left-handed anymore. Said they can't do as well. I just got one thing to say about that: they never saw you.

LOST IN THE DARK

by

RAYMOND ABNEY

Henderson and I were drinking tequila, licking the salt off the backs of our hands, squeezing the lime into our mouths and then slurping the tequila out of the bottle. We were sitting outside on my patio watching the sun go down and talking. It was one of those rare, soft, sweet evenings that make people want to sit outside and talk with no lights on so they don't have to look at each other's eyes. Henderson comes over to drink and talk every once in awhile, but I never really thought that I knew him very well. He lives just a few houses away and our kids are about the same age, so I see him at school and ball games and sometimes at the grocery store. We were both in the Corps, so I guess that makes him think that we share something, and I guess we do. He was talking about the war, and I could tell by the way he talked that what he was saying was true, not mostly true but happened to someone else, like so many stories about the war.

Henderson's a big guy with a bit of a beer belly and long red hair the way hippies used to wear it, parted in the middle and always falling in his eyes. I had never thought about him having any faults, other than drinking too much and staring at my wife's breasts. He seems to always be drinking—usually Lucky Lager beer, but occasionally red wine from a jug, or if someone will drink with him, the hard stuff. He sits on his front porch and drinks all weekend sometimes, greeting everyone who walks by, waving at people in cars. If he doesn't know you are watching, though, you can see him staring straight ahead, scowling almost, gripping the beer bottle on the arm of the chair.

That night he was really relaxed. We had talked about the Dodgers and about the kids' Little League team and about mortgage rates and a little about politics, but nothing very heavy. The sun had been down for a long time, and I could barely make out his face against the jasmine bush he was sitting next to.

"Getting dark," I said.

"Yeah," said Henderson, taking another sip. He was staring out towards the fence, not moving, barely breathing. "Not dark like Nam, though. Nothing that dark, huh?"

"I was never there," I said.

"You weren't there? You were in the Corps though. Right?"

"Yeah, but I never left Pendleton."

I heard him take the salt shaker and shake some onto his hand. Then he felt for the lime, licked his hand, and squeezed the lime into his mouth, slurping softly. I handed him the bottle and he took a long drink, swallowing twice. Then he sat back in the squeaky lawn chair and took a deep breath, exhaling noisily through his nose.

"I killed a guy over there on a night like this."

"Don't worry about it," I said. "Lots of guys had to kill while they were over there. It don't mean nothin' "

"No. I mean I killed one of our guys. Sort of a friend of mine."

I sat for a long time staring at my feet, at where I knew my feet would be, if I could see them. What could I say? I wanted to know, but then I didn't. I reached out to put my hand on his shoulder, but in the dark I missed and brushed his cheek, my hand coming to rest on his collar. He leaned his head over and rubbed his cheek on the back of my hand, caressing it, almost. He gave it a sort of squeeze, and then straightened his head. I could tell he was looking at me.

"It wasn't like I was mad at him or anything. It was just . . . necessary. He was going to die anyway. He was almost dead. Do you want to hear about it or not?" He was already plenty drunk, and I didn't want him to start crying or get violent or anything, but I wanted to hear the story. I listened as he shook, licked, squeezed and slurped another shot.

"It wasn't any big deal. I mean, I didn't enjoy it or anything like that, but it didn't bother me much at the time because like I said, it was necessary."

"Why?" I asked.

"Because he was about to get us all killed anyway. I just didn't have any choice."

"How did this happen?" I still wasn't sure whether he would tell me, and I wasn't sure how much longer he would be able to talk with so much tequila.

He sighed deeply. "Well, we were out on patrol one day. It was really hot, you know how it gets over there. And we were up near Hue, a few months before the Tet offensive. The VC and NVA regulars had both been moving into our area for a couple of months, and we knew that something was going to happen. That is, those of us out in the field knew it. Those idiots sitting in Saigon pumping out orders didn't know jack shit. So they had us going outside the perimeter every day looking for the enemy. Fuck, we knew they were out there. All those pricks had to do was ask us. We could hear them every night out there moving around. We'd send up a flare and fire a few rounds just to see if they'd fire back, but we'd never see them. It's weird. The little fuckers would hide out in the jungle all day and we'd hear them at night just outside our perimeter setting booby traps and snooping around, but you could never see them."

Henderson shifted in his chair and leaned his head back, looking at the sky. "It's funny," he said. "Here you can't see very many stars, and yet it's light compared to over there. Over there you could look up and see millions of stars, millions. And you'd think that that many stars would light up everything, but it would be so pitch black you couldn't see anything. I mean nothing.

"So anyway we were going out on patrol nearly every day, just looking around. Sometimes we'd find their booby traps. They aren't really that hard to find once you know what to look for. They'd always try to stay one jump ahead of us, you know, like trying something new. But we'd catch on and then they'd have to find something else. It was like a game or something. But that wasn't the worst part. I mean, you were nervous out there all the time, not really knowing if they had found something new and you were going to get blown away. But the worst part was the feeling that they were watching everything you did. I really feel like they were watching us all day, trying to figure out how we could be so stupid as to come out into their territory every day just to find their booby traps and disarm them, just so they could put them back the next night.

"So we were out there this one day, and like I said, it was fucking hot. And we hadn't found one sign of the little bastards, nothing. And that made everyone even more nervous. So we started back towards base late in the afternoon, but in plenty of time to make it back before dark. See, you didn't dare try to come back through the perimeter after dark. Those people just inside the wire were so shaky they'd shoot at anything, even if it sounded like it was from Brooklyn. If you stayed out until dark, you might as well stay out all night. It was a lot safer than trying to make it back through the line.

"Anyway we were coming down through this little valley about four clicks from the base. We'd been through this place a hundred times before. We'd gone up through not six hours before. But it was different that afternoon. For one thing, it was quiet. Real quiet. I mean there's not usually a lot of noise in the goddamn jungle, not like you see in the movies with monkeys howling and all that, but it was even quieter that day, and fucking hot. And we're coming down this valley, not in any kind of formation, 'cause the trail was pretty narrow, but just sort of straggling along about five yards apart. And it was so quiet. Just the noise of men walking, shuffling through this dust that was about a foot deep. I was looking at this guy's feet in front of me. Every step he took was like he was going to sink into this dust up to his hips, but his boot would stop and then it would start back up again and you'd think that it would leave a big hole, but the dust just sort of filled back in again and by the time my foot got there it was like no one had ever walked there before. All I could do was watch his goddamn feet. And that's all I could hear, too. It was like the sound was magnified. There was this 'pfoof' when his foot went into the dust, then a 'whoosh' when it came out, then, I swear to God, I could hear the dust falling back into the hole, sort of an avalanche kind of sound. I guess I was just goofing, because I was so scared. I knew something was going to happen, I just knew it. Where's the salt shaker?"

I felt around on the TV tray that was between us until I found the shaker, and handed it to him. I could hear him going through the ritual and waited until I heard him swallow and sigh. "And did it?" I asked.

"What?"

"Did something happen? Right then?"

"Yeah. Yeah, I was just watching this guy's feet, and all of a sudden, he dives off to the side. Then I started hearing all the rest of it. This guy named Daniels from Louisiana had tripped a wire across the trail and set off a frag grenade. He had just caught up with the Indian to bum a cigarette. The Indian would have seen it, but that fucking Daniels was talking to him. Indian and I came to the platoon on the same day, so we had been through all this shit together. He was from some little town in South Dakota, on the reservation. Just a kid, but real tough. Everybody thought he was stupid because he never said much, but he had this way of just looking at something until he got it figured out, then he would do what had to be done. I haven't seen him since that day, but I loved him. I was closer to him than I've ever been to anybody.

"So this guy Daniels caught it pretty bad. Indian had dived off the trail as soon as he heard the pin pop out of the grenade, but he still got a lot of shit in his left foot and leg. And as soon as the grenade went off, we started getting some machine gun fire. It was just one of those piddly-ass little French guns, but it sure sounded loud in that little valley. Daniels was screaming for his mother, and someone was yelling for the corpsman and everyone else was shooting at the machine gun. Or maybe just shooting. I think about half the people in a situation like that, especially the new guys, just shoot off their weapons into the air, just to feel like they're doing something. Half the time you can't tell where the fire is coming from anyway. Everybody's too scared to think. I know I was scared shitless every time something like that happened.

"And then all of a sudden it just stopped. The machine gun had stopped, and everybody quit firing back, and it got really quiet again, just like before. We just laid there and waited, nobody saying anything, just waiting for something else to happen. I was laying on the side of the trail, sort of halfway in this ditch full of slimy water, but with my head and shoulders still on the dirt. And when I raised my head to look around, I noticed that the dirt was dark where my face had been. That's the first I knew I'd been hit, too. I'd caught a couple of fragments in my cheek. One of them had gone right through. It left two little holes. You've probably noticed the scars here on my right cheek."

"No," I said, "I've never noticed."

"Sure you have. There's a little scar here at the corner of my mouth and a bigger one a little further back. There's another further back, but my sideburn hides it."

"I guess I've never noticed."

"Sure you have."

We just sat for a few minutes and breathed the cool night air. Someone was doing the dishes across the alley, clattering the plates and running water too fast. There was a TV on somewhere droning the late night news. I thought that was all of the story I was going to hear, but Henderson breathed deeply, exhaling loudly and slowly, and continued.

"I didn't feel anything. Just sort of a numb feeling on the side of my face. I started thinking that I was maybe hit somewhere else and didn't know it yet, so I felt all over my body. I started at my feet and just felt myself all over, and I was OK.

"After awhile, when we saw that nothing else was going to happen, people started talking and moving around a little bit. The word came back that Indian and Daniels had been hit, so I got up and started walking down towards the front of the formation. At first everyone was telling me to get down, that there was going to be more action, but when nothing happened, they just let me go. The corpsman had pulled Indian up out of the ditch and had him leaning up against a mound of dirt and was doing something to Daniels. Like I say, Daniels was pretty messed up. He had caught most of the shit, and one of his legs was pretty much gone. The doc had cut his shirt off and was sort of dabbing at all the wounds on his belly. His leg was just a mess. There was bone sticking out, and it was just kind of twisted back under the other one. I just knew he wouldn't last long. He was an OK guy, just stupid.

"I looked at Indian and he looked scared. He was biting his lip and just staring up at the sky. There was blood seeping out of his boot, and a few bloody spots on his pantleg. I was glad he wasn't hurt bad, but I knew he was going home, and I guess it sort of made me mad. We had been through it all together, and he was going home and I was going to have to stay in that fucking place and eat shit and maybe get killed sometime and all I would have is a bunch of new guys like Daniels. So I sat down in the dirt beside him and didn't say anything, and he looked up at me and I could tell he was thinking the same thing, and we both just started to cry. You think that's funny? We both just cried like babies.

"So after awhile the lieutenant comes over. He was a real prick. From Annapolis, you know what I mean? A real candyass prick. And he says to get up and move out so we can make it back to the base by nightfall. He had called the chopper, but it wasn't there yet, and he says since I can walk, I'm going back in with them. I just told him to fuck off. Just like that. He started giving me some shit, and I told him if he wanted to shoot me for disobeying an order, I'd give him my gun to do it with, and otherwise to get out of my sight. He pissed and moaned and finally said he would take the corpsman and leave me to help haul Indian and Daniels out to the chopper when it came, and I told him to go ahead and do it. So the corpsman came over and gave Indian a shot of morphine and me some pills of some kind and a wad of cotton for my cheek, and then they moved Daniels and Indian and me down the trail about a hundred yards to the edge of a rice paddy where the chopper would set down. And then they all left. That candyass just left us there. I probably could have had him court-martialed, but I didn't want to stir up any trouble.

"So we just sat and waited for the chopper to come. The sun went down over the hills and I started to get a little nervous. And then it started getting dark and I kept thinking, If it comes right now we'll be OK and If it comes in the next five minutes we'll be OK. And the sonofabitch never did come. I've never been so scared in my life as I was watching it get darker and darker and when I finally knew it was too dark for the chopper to come. I could just see the VC stumbling across us in the dark and cutting us up like dog meat.

"I moved Daniels and Indian across the ditch into some bushes so at least we wouldn't be on the trail. Daniels was unconscious by then, so he was just dead weight. Every once in a while he would moan and groan, but he didn't even wake up when I carried him across the ditch. I don't know why he didn't just die then. I tried talking to Indian, but he was pretty out of it from the morphine. So we just waited. I could hear all kinds of things moving around in the dark. I could tell it was animals, but then I heard some people walk by. It must have been about four or five of them, and they weren't wearing boots. You could tell they were barefoot by the sound their feet made in the dirt. They were walking along whispering to each other real low, I guess to keep track of one another. I thought my heart was going to pound right out of my chest.

"And then everything was OK for awhile. I just sat and listened to the animals moving around and tried to not think about how bad a situation I was in. Then Daniels's morphine started to wear off and he started to make these funny little noises, like a cat meowing or something. Indian was awake then, too. He said he was cold, so I covered them both up with my shelter half. I was sitting there wondering what to do next when I heard this sort of a whistle. A real soft one, sort of like this: wheet. And it wasn't like any other sound I'd heard that night. Is there another drink in that bottle?"

I found the bottle on the grass between us and handed it over to him. He took the last of it and dropped the empty bottle back on the grass. "So I crawled over and put my hand over Daniels's mouth and we listened, but all I could hear was the blood pounding in my head. After awhile that quieted down and I started to hear the footsteps again, only more of them this time. And Daniels was starting to get noisier, kind of whimpering, and he was jerking all over. I was laying on top of him to hold him down but he just kept jerking and whimpering and thrashing, so I eased my bayonet out of its scabbord and . . . just . . . slid it up under his ribs. Into his heart. I . . . I didn't . . ."

Henderson was sobbing quietly and privately. I sat and stared at the blackness.

He straightened up in his chair after awhile and cleared his throat. "The chopper came as soon as it was light. I helped them load Daniels and the Indian and we all went to the field hospital. Daniels had so many holes in him that I'm sure nobody ever knew. Except Indian. They had given him another shot of morphine when I said goodbye to him, but I could tell he knew. They flew him out to a hospital ship and I never saw him again. Anything left in that bottle?"

"No," I said. "But there's another one in the house. You want me to go get it?"

"No," said Henderson. "No. Just stay here with me."

SPENDING THEIR GOLDEN YEARS

by

IRVING HALPERN

I looked across the table at my mother who had just sat down for dinner, as she had on so many other evenings during the ten years she had been living with me and my family. I was a little nervous—and not very hungry. I was trying to find a way to tell my 79-year-old mother that, upon the advice of our family doctor, I was seriously thinking of a convalescent home for her.

From my mother, my eyes went to my wife, Martha, now in her late thirties. She was still as beautiful as the day I met her—with that same flamboyant look that charmed me in our courting days. When I visited Dr. Schwartz that morning, he informed me that not only was Mother's arthritic condition getting progressively worse, but that Martha herself was not up to par physically; and again he brought up the subject of sending Mother to a nursing home.

"I can only repeat what I have told you before Joe: your mother will soon be needing 'round the clock professional care, and a good nursing home is the only place she can get it. As I see it, you have no other choice." He rose, walked over to me, put his arm over my shoulder and continued: "It isn't the end of the world you know." Smiling, he said: "She may actually enjoy being with folks her own age, people she can talk to about old times."

"For all you know she may be secretly wishing for a chance to leave your house. Ten years under the same roof, well, maybe it's been a little too much, and too long for her."

I hesitated and wiped my eyes. "Hell, Doc, I can't do it. I can't tell

42

my mother, 'sorry, Mom—you're too much trouble and bother, we've got to put you away with the rest of the old folks.'

"I know you're trying to make me feel better," I said, swallowing hard, "but I don't think I could live with myself if I placed Mother in a home. Before Father died he made me promise always to take good care of Mama. Martha would feel guilty too, I know it."

Dr. Schwartz nodded and paused before replying, choosing his words carefully. "Look at it this way," he said, "you are keeping your promise if you see that she is getting the professional care that she is entitled to. Anything less is actually depriving her of what she needs."

I returned to my office, and many times during the day thought over the doctor's words. Dr. Schwartz was more than our doctor; he was a family friend. I honestly respected his advice. The only problem was whether I could accept it. Sitting at the dinner table this evening, my heart was heavy with that sick feeling of guilt at the thought of having to tell my mother what Dr. Schwartz suggested.

I had long known that this problem would come up someday, but still I was confused and having trouble coping. I was able to accept Dr. Schwartz's advice logically but not emotionally.

I knew that if I mentioned a nursing home Mama would feel unwanted. Undoubtedly she would get the impression that she was in the way—and that with her absence her room could be used for Martha's studio and for her paintings. I didn't want that. I loved my mother, as did Martha and our little son Mark. Martha always regarded my mother as an honored guest, not an intruder.

At dinner that evening I imagined that my mother's eyes were on me, eyes filled with concern as they always were at the slightest change in my attitude. At this point I began to think how we would feel being away from her, and unable to share her words of wisdom.

After going to bed, Martha and I were both restless. My last waking thought was an impulsive decision—Rabbi Fisher. Yes, why not. I would go see him in the morning and explain the situation. I would ask for his help and advice.

Rabbi Fisher had been a friend of the family for many years. It was passing the buck, but I somehow lacked the courage to do anything else.

The next day, after explaining why I had come to see him, the rabbi said, "You know our biggest problems in life have a very strange way of working themselves out. What you must keep in mind, Joe, is that Dr. Schwartz is recommending what is best for your mother. By the way," he continued, "I'm the one who feels guilty for not calling on your mother in so long a time." He then looked at the calendar on his desk and added, "Give her a message for me. Tell her if she comes to the synagogue this Saturday I promise to come for a visit next Wednesday."

"Great," I said, and immediately felt better. Martha and Mother both liked the rabbi, and I knew that they would not mind him coming for dinner. I made up my mind that I would come home early and help with the preparations; it would be a small price to pay to have someone ease the blow for me, to sort of lay the ground work.

That Saturday was one of mother's good days. By the time we were ready to leave for the synagogue, Mother was walking easily, insisting she did not need her cane, which I put in the car anyway.

I sat in the pew between Martha and my mother, my mind wandering. I listened abstractedly to the sermon, thinking of it only as time to kill until the rabbi would see me at the door to confirm our dinner arrangement. Quite abruptly I was made aware of words spoken by Rabbi Fisher. I sat upright and began to listen intently. "Naturally, all children—sons and daughters—feel an extreme responsibility to their aging parents. But often they are blind to the wishes and desires of these elderly people—they become so obsessed with their own importance in deciding and dictating what is best for the parent that they fail to ask the parent how he or she would like to spend their so-called Golden Years." The remainder of the sermon dealt compassionately with the delicate concerns of families and old age. I began to realize how little I had considered the possiblity that my mother might have needs that she had difficulty expressing to me.

Things went along as usual between Saturday and Wednesday, except that I felt more relaxed. I had lost the tenseness that had disrupted my days and nights following my visits to Dr. Schwartz. Slowly but firmly I decided to accept the rabbi's philosophy that all problems have a way of working themselves out.

All through the soup and salad courses the rabbi's conversation was light and impersonal. As I began to carve the roast I wondered what was going to happen next. Then my mother suddenly said, "I hate to interrupt you, Rabbi, but before we start on Martha's beautiful roast I'd like to make an announcement, something I hope all of you, the dearest and most important people in my life, will agree to."

All eyes focused on my mother. She paused, smiled, and took a very long breath. "First, I want to say that I love all of you." She said this slowly and softly, wiping away a tear that was starting to form. "I've been very, very happy here as part of my son's family."

She turned to smile at the rabbi, "but since listening to your beautiful sermon last Saturday I've been thinking, and have decided that perhaps you were right. I should have the privilege of making my own choice as to where I want to live the rest of my years, and I've come to the conclusion that I would rather be in a nursing home, with people of my own age who I can talk to and play cards with."

She then reached over and tousled Mark's hair, "Not that I don't enjoy playing rummy with my grandson, but I always played pinochle with his grandfather, and I miss it very much."

My mother ended her announcement quite abruptly by looking at me and saying, "Joe, will you go out one of these days and find me a nursing home?"

I nearly carved my finger instead of the roast. Those next few minutes were happy and excited ones, and none of the others saw the wink and the smile that the rabbi gave me.

The next morning Martha and I started the chore of checking out places on the list that Dr. Schwartz gave me. The first two, both within the range of my mother's pension, were overcrowded and understaffed. The buildings were old and badly in need of repairs. The attendants seemed bored and non-committal in response to most of our questions. Just looking at those places depressed us both. But the third one, called "The Old Pines", 75 miles from home and set in a grove of stately old pines, seemed like just the place we were looking for.

We knew it the moment we drove through the gates. As we drove up to the administration building we both knew that it would be more costly than what Mother expected to pay, but we decided long before we met the director, a Mrs. Spencer, that we would make up the difference in money without letting mother know.

I was very eager and excited to get home and give mother the many brochures describing this nursing home as well as our own personal impressions. Mrs. Spencer had also suggested a visit, adding that all potential guests do this, and that we were all invited for lunch the following Sunday.

About ten days after the necessary mental and physical examinations had been completed, Mother was registered as a permanent guest.

The house was rather quiet after Mother left. During the next six months I took Martha and Mark for weekend visits to see Mother, or whenever Mother scheduled the days. Sometimes we took her for a ride whenever she felt up to it. Occasionally we stopped at a small inn to have dinner and enjoy the singing by the waiters. On weekends a pianist urged the diners to join in and sing the old-time songs she played.

"I really enjoy having dinner here," Mother remarked one evening, "and I do have a friend at the Home who would love to join us sometime." I told her that another guest wouldn't present any problem, and that I'd be happy to have her friend come with us any time. I was extremely pleased that Mother had found a friend there.

On our drive back from The Old Pines one night, Martha was rather quiet. When I asked her why, she replied, "I don't know, Joe. I have a certain feeling, something that I just can't explain. There is something on Mama's mind.

After Martha's remark I waited subconsciously each night for the phone to ring, for a call from my mother asking that on our next visit we come prepared to take her back home.

Finally, about two weeks later, a call did come. It was a week before our next scheduled visit. Mother's first words were: "Joseph, I hope you and Martha won't be too upset." She so seldom called me Joseph, reserving such formality only for the most important of events. I prepared myself for the worst, breaking into a sweat.

"I won't waste words," she went on, "but I have met a gentleman friend here, and we want to get married. Could you arrange to bring Rabbi Fisher with you next Sunday? We'd like all of you to help us with the arrangements. Joseph—Joseph—are you there? Do you hear me?"

"Yes, yes, Mama, I hear you. Congratulations!" I fairly shouted this into the phone and then, cupping the receiver in my palm, called out to Martha in the kitchen. "MARTHA—MARTHA—get in here quick, you won't believe what Mama has to tell you!"

I smiled to myself and tried to calm down while I waited for Martha to get to the phone.

TRANSFER

by

Frank Ware

This morning I felt good. It wasn't because anything was going right. Both my cars were in shops and I had just dropped off the second at Bernard's. Bernard was a middle-aged Austrian whose accent was so thick I could hardly understand him. I would come in the morning and explain to him what I thought was wrong, and when I came back in the evening he'd tell me what went wrong. I never understood a thing he told me, but he did good work and was cheap.

After dropping off the car I had to walk a couple of blocks to the bus stop. It was eight-thirty in the morning and some old lady was out mowing her lawn already. Her lawn was the size of a postage stamp. Good thing, because all she had was a regular old mower. You didn't have to worry about running over the cord with an old mower.

I got to the bus stop. Across the street was a coffee shop, The Kozy Koffee Shop. I hadn't eaten yet, and besides, I wanted a paper. I stood in front of the racks deciding which paper I wanted while this guy was trying to kick over a Harley. He was right in front of the Chronicle rack. The Harley was not kicking over. I didn't buy a paper.

I went inside and sat down at a booth. In the corner behind me, next to the door, was a black man. I heard him say, "Hola, amigo, que tal?" to the busboy. The busboy did not respond. I ordered.

The black man asked, "Could I have another cup of coffee please? Thank you." The waitress was polite to him, as he was to her.

A few minutes later a construction worker came in and sat down at the counter. He faced both of us. I was reading a book I happened to have with me. "Hey, hey you," I heard the black man say. I did not want to

47

talk to him or anyone else. "Hey . . . hey buddy." I looked out the window. A bus came and went. I looked at my watch. It was ten after nine.

"Yeah, what do you want?" the construction worker asked.

"Could you please get me a cup of coffee?"

To my surprise the construction worker got up, went over to the waitress station and picked up the pot. This didn't make any sense to me. I was waiting for a waitress to run up to him and scold him for picking up the coffee pot. I had seen waitresses become very possessive of coffee pots before. I waited. He poured the coffee. I could hear him pour.

"Thank you. I have to drink a lot of coffee." The way the man was talking, the way he spoke and the way he was treated by people and the fact that he drank lots of coffee, I surmised that this man was mad. I had only caught a glance of him as I walked in. He did not interest me so I did not pay attention to him at all, and I did not see anything different about him. I wondered why madmen drank so much coffee.

"I have to drink coffee to counter-balance the medication they give me. It makes me drowsy," he explained.

That's right. Those poor people are stoned on styllazine and thorozine all the time.

"Thank you," he said again. He was certainly a polite madman.

The construction worker put the coffee pot back in its place and walked back to his place at the counter. The waitress walked by him, touched him on the arm, and smiled. "Thanks, that was very nice of you." The construction worker looked up and shrugged.

My order came.

A few minutes later the black man got up to leave. He went to the counter to pay for his gallon of coffee. He reached in his pockets. I looked over. He was wearing red and white checkered Big Boy pants held up by suspenders made for a smaller man. He had trouble getting change out of his pockets. The waitress waited patiently. He pulled out some change. This is when I noticed that he had no hands.

They both looked down at the change he had put on the counter. She looked up at him and said. "That's okay. It's on me."

He said, "Thank you very much," and left.

Some people walked up to the cash register, smiling and talking to each other. They were talking about him.

I looked out across the street and saw the red and white checkered Big Boy overalls sitting on the bench, waiting for the same bus I would be waiting for. I thought maybe I should have another cup of coffee and let him take the next bus in peace—just to avoid confronting him. With all the experience I've had talking to mad people I've learned it was better to avoid them. But I felt differently about him. I didn't want another cup of coffee. I got up and paid the bill, left, and walked across the street. He was sitting in the middle of the bench. He wore wraparound shades. I sat down.

"Hi," he said.

"Hello," I said.

"Would you like to come to my house? I live in East Palo Alto. They have security there. I'm into security."

"No thanks. I am very busy. I have a lot of things to do," I answered. He nodded. "Do you need a job? I can get you a job."

"No thanks. I have a job already," I said.

"Oh that's right. You're busy. What kind of job do you have?"

"I'm a mailman."

"Oh." He looked down. He didn't like me being a mailman.

"Do you have a dollar?"

"No," I smiled the lie at him.

"I'm sorry." He put his head in what was left of his hands. "I shouldn't have asked you for money. All I want to be is your friend."

I didn't answer this. The bus came.

"How much is the bus now?" I asked.

"Do you mean for you?" He was reaching in his pockets again.

"Yes."

"Fifty cents."

I walked up the steps leading to the bus driver. "Is the fare fifty cents?"

"Yes," she said.

I put the change in and walked back to an empty seat. The black man sat down in front of me, a couple of rows up. He sat on the seat that is turned sideways because of the wheelwell. We drove on.

I looked about the bus and sized everybody up. Old ladies, foreigners and a couple of students. A young woman got up and moved to the back. She was pretty. I was surprised that I had overlooked her. I attributed it to the fact that I had a preconception that only old ladies and foreigners use the bus. In cities, as everyone knows, everyone uses the public transport. In the suburbs, not having a car was as bad as not having hands. My friend looked back at me.

"Do you shave yourself?"

Everyone looked at me for the answer.

I laughed. "Well, I didn't shave today, but yes, I do shave."

"Can you shave me? I want to shave my beard."

"I don't think I can. I'm a busy person."

"That's right," he said. "You are a busy person. I want to have my beard shaved."

"It's a nice beard." I looked out the window. How come whenever your car screws up you notice all the garages you pass? We went past the Army-Navy surplus, past the fire department. Clean and sober people were standing in front of the fire department. We went past the house that a kid who had only one arm lived in. He was dancing to no music as he always had done when I went past. He looked happy. He always looked happy, but until then I had never noticed.

The man that needed the shave and an old man from somewhere else, like the Philippines, got off the bus. The man that needed a shave asked for a transfer. The driver gave it to him. As we drove away I saw him talk to the old man. The old man smiled.

The bus turned the corner and drove a mile or so. I pressed the yellow strip that rang the bell that notified the driver I wanted off. She stopped. I asked for a transfer and got off.

I walked up to the bench, sat down, and stared at the highway. A woman was walking towards me. She was attractive. I stared. She had white blonde hair and a fair complexion. It was the same woman I'd seen on the first bus. Her head was down. She walked behind the bench. I felt good. Then she turned and sat down at the other end of the bench. All of a sudden I felt very self-conscious. I sat up straight and stared at a point about half-way in the turning lane. I had tunnel vision. I kept turning to look at her. It wasn't obvious. She would be looking down, and I would focus in like any jerk. She'd glance at me and in a moment I would panic and jump back to the turning lane.

All of a sudden I noticed the traffic. The drivers, the men, they were staring. The stares would barely miss me and land on the woman next to me. At first I became nervous, because it just wasn't five or ten. It was as much as four lanes could hold. The faces were all different but their expression was one. She was looking down. Then for some reason a grin grew on my face. There were fat rednecks down from their trucks. The businessmen looked from large Buicks. The long hairs stared from dirty windows. They were all isolated from each other but on this point they all agreed: that girl next to me was worth looking at.

I wanted to talk to the woman. I felt it was my obligation, because I felt apologetic about the behavior of my side. But my tongue froze. It was hard to get the first word out, but I thought it was worth the effort. "Excuse me." She looked up. She had the lightest blue eyes I had ever seen. Her cheeks were just right, high but smooth. Her face glowed with warmth. I was broken. I looked at the street for help to find something to say. "I know this is gonna sound strange . . . I shouldn't say this . . . and it's gonna sound weird . . ." With an introduction like that I knew I had her attention. Maybe she thought *I* was a madman. My mind was trying to back out of the situation, but my hand helped out. I started waving at the road. She followed the motions my hand made. ". . . but do you notice that all the dudes that drive by stare at you?" She laughed a kind laugh and looked down.

"You make me feel embarrassed." She looked up and smiled. She was warm, unlike the people in the street.

"Sorry, I know I shouldn't have said it, but go ahead and look for yourself." I pointed out to the street. She looked out. An old man turned his head. She looked away and rubbed her eyes. She laughed to herself. I ran out of things to say. I looked out to see how many people were looking. A car in the near lane slowed down. A guy with a beard hung out of an empty window. His hands cupped his mouth and he hooted. She laughed and looked away from me. Then she turned back and said, "Now you've made me self-conscious about it."

"It's true though. I've never seen it from this angle. It looks totally absurd. Does this happen to you all the time?" She smiled. "I mean, do you like it or what?"

She smiled again. Her smile was worth a lot to me. "Well, I don't know. It makes me feel good I guess. . . . Like sometimes I even stare back, but sometimes I wish that they had never stared at me. It depends on who's doing it, I guess."

"Yeah, but it feels . . . I don't know. It feels . . . it feels really impersonal."

She looked away. This time she didn't smile, she just shrugged. The shrug didn't have any value for me.

"I mean, look out there. I'll try to keep count." That turned her around again. Then total disaster: an old man walked up and sat between us. He was the butcher's brother; he sure knew how to cut us. All of us stared forward. Men kept looking back. I leaned around the old man and said, "That's three."

The old man looked at me and said something about the economy. He went on comparing today with some forty-odd years ago. He was in full gear. All I could do was nod.

Then, wouldn't you know it: the goddam bus showed up. We all got up. She went before me. She sat in a seat by herself. I handed the driver my transfer and walked back. The seat next to her was empty, but so were many others. She might think I am trying to pick her up, and she has probably had enough of that for one day. I wanted to talk to her, but I walked by and sat down two seats behind her. I wanted to say something but didn't.

Three miles later she got up and said goodbye. She pushed the back door open. The bus pulled away. I wanted to look back, but I didn't.

THE ENEMY WITHIN

by

L.W. PETERSON

Somehow it didn't work out exactly the way I had it planned. I thought I had taken everything into account: the proper time of night, the explosives, the radio frequency, the transmitter. I had enough experience in Nam as an explosives expert; there had been only six others like me. None better, they said.

But something went wrong, something for which I couldn't have planned. Something out of the ordinary. How was I to know that patrol car would drive down the street? It wasn't scheduled to be there. I know it wasn't! I had watched that street for three weeks straight. How was I supposed to know they would drive up just as I pushed the button? They had me against the side of my car when I heard the people inside the house screaming. Two charges, one in front and one in back. There was no way for them to escape. Well, they deserved it. I warned them time and time again to keep their dog inside the house. . . .

BUT NO!, they just had to let that mutt chase me all the way down the street. Well, he's charcoal now.

"Watch your tail!" that's what I had been told. A thousand times I had been told that. It still echoes inside my head. I thought I had learned. "You're dead meat, lieutenant!" That's what Colonel Garvey said after he caught me from behind. He was in the process of slitting my throat with a knife at the time. "Everyone is out to get you! Don't trust anyone!" Those were the mottos I lived by.

After a few months in Nam I got so I could feel someone behind me. But there's a fine line between being alert and being paranoid. When you started seeing things behind every bush, every tree, that's when they shipped you home.

I thought I left the enemy back there. Who would have thought that my own people would turn against me. But they did, and I couldn't let them get away with it. I had been through too much already. I thought that my little plan would teach them all a lesson. A lesson they wouldn't forget.

At first I thought the people on my mail route just didn't think. They would move their mailbox, hide it behind a bush. Sometimes it took me ten minutes just to find it. Or they would take it down entirely. What was I supposed to do with their mail then? Or they would let the ice build up on their sidewalks and steps. It was like walking through a mine field. Like I said, people just didn't think.

But later, strange things started happening. People started letting their dogs out just before I got to their houses. I know they had just let them out because there were no dogs around when I drove my truck past and parked it at the end of the block. They must have seen me coming. They must have been waiting for me. They must have been looking out their windows to see me drive by. They know what time I deliver their mail, it's about the same time every day. They were out to get me, that's all there was to it!

Well, they started this war, not me. Just remember, there are no rules in war. Just because I'm in this P.O.W. camp now doesn't mean that the war is over —not yet. I escaped from that camp in Nam and I can get out of here, too. And when I do, I have a few more battle plans in mind.

SAVED BY SIN

by

RAYMOND ABNEY

It was two weeks after his tenth birthday when Harry fell into the gravel pit. He was supposed to be walking from his grandmother's house, where he went after school every day, to his own house on the other side of the highway. It was the first day he had ever been allowed to go by himself. His older brother Jake had to stay after school and scrub urinals for smoking in the bathroom, and Harry had begged his grandmother to let him go on home by himself.

It had been a rainy spring and there were puddles of icy, muddy water everywhere. In order to get to his house he had to walk through a corrugated culvert that ran beneath the four-lane highway near the water tower. The bottom of the culvert was covered with sandy dirt and a few inches of water, and Harry knew that he had to walk through spread-legged, the way Jake had shown him. It had not been the same, entering the culvert without Jake, peering in, straining to see the glow of light halfway through where the culvert had a slight bend that hid the other end. Harry yelled into the darkness to scare away anything inside, and had recoiled at the loudness and the echo of his own voice. He had thrown a fist-sized rock in and jumped back from its noisy, hollow clatter, but, satisfied that he had purged the culvert of demons, had stepped into the wet darkness. When he got to the middle he looked back and was frightened by his shadow, which had jumped behind him and stood hovering over his left shoulder like some evil spirit come out to grab him around the neck and choke the life out of him. He had let out a little gasp and, forgetting the water in the bottom of the culvert, had run to the other end and emerged with wet shoes and wide eyes into the bright light and cold wind.

Most children would have been frightened enough by such an experience to stay out of trouble for the rest of the day, but Harry was one of those who, when he did something stupid or dangerous, felt compelled to follow it up with something even more stupid or dangerous. Thus it was that Harry found himself staring down into the gravel pit, opening and closing his hands and breathing hard and fast, having run all the way from the culvert, across a plowed but not yet planted field, under a barbed wire fence with two strands missing, past the Danger—No Trespassing signs, to the edge of the pit, where he stared down at the muddy water. There was usually only a little water in the pit, just enough to make a good splash when rocks were thrown into it. But the rains had raised the water level, which in turn seemed to raise the bottom of the pit, making it seem much less threatening than when the bottom was fifty feet from the edge on which Harry was standing.

Harry bent over to pick up a rock, but because he was dizzy from running, or because of the books under his arm, or because of the looseness of the gravel—or just because—he fell forward and rolled and slid and tumbled down the side of the pit into the cold water.

"God damn," said Harry, when his head came up out of the water. "Sonofabitch." He had heard Jake and his father say both words many times before, but he had never tried them out. They sounded appropriate, and he was proud of himself for having used them so correctly. But there was a hollow ring to them: perhaps, he thought, because there was no one to hear.

The water was ice cold, and he tried at once to climb out, but found that he could pull himself out only to about his waist before the weight of his body on the slippery gravel pulled him back into the water. He tried digging in the gravel to find a handhold, but found that it was gravel as far as he could dig. He tried going up the bank sideways, but found that as soon as he lifted his leg out of the water, he slipped back in. He tried pulling gravel down into the water under his legs, thinking that it would build up under him and he would be able to crawl out, but the gravel slipped far down below his legs. He scuttled along the bank looking for better footing but found none, and came back to the place where he had fallen in.

And then young Harry Hopkins cried. He cried with the sorrow of a small boy facing certain death. He cried until he was sobbing uncontrollably, snot smearing across his wet cheek, his mouth and throat thick with metallic-tasting mucus. And then he yelled, screamed actually, until his voice was no more than a hoarse whisper, a croak in the wind that blew down into the pit and across his back, making his lips blue and his teeth chatter.

Harry rested for a few minutes, feeling the numbness creeping up his legs, feeling the stomach cramps begin. And then he began to pray. He had never prayed before. His family did not go to church, but he had stayed overnight with Dallas Rhoden, whose family prayed at every meal, when they went to bed and when they woke up, and every time there was thunder or they heard about someone being sick. He prayed the way they prayed, aloud and in as strong and clear a voice as he could manage.

"Dear Lord, please allow this young boy to be delivered from this . . . this danger, this pit of water. Please let him live so that he might grow up big and strong. We ask this in God's name, amen." He repeated the prayer several times in slightly different forms, always emphasizing how young he was and how much he wanted to grow up. Then he tried climbing out again. He made several determined tries, and once got completely out of the water, but slipped back down each time. He prayed again, almost demanding this time to be delivered. "Dear Lord, You promised to take care of little children. The Bible says You will." (Harry was not at all sure that the Bible said so, but he thought that it sounded believable.) "I've been praying to You for an hour and You should help me now if You want me to grow up and be a good Christian." Harry tried again and again to climb out, putting all his strength into forcing a foothold or a handhold in the loose gravel. He growled and sobbed as he pulled at the crumbling surface, breaking off his fingernails and causing his hands to start bleeding. He stopped trying to climb and looked at his hands in horror. He started to cry again and held his hands up to the sky. "Now look what You've done, You son of a bitch," he screamed. "I'm going to die and You don't even care." In his anger Harry renewed his efforts, scrambling even more frantically against the gravel. He got farther up the side than he ever had before, but as he felt himself start to slide back down he gave up hope completely and began sobbing again, letting himself slide head first into the cold, welcome water, hoping to drown. He slid further down into the water, his face resting on the cold, hard gravel. He knew that his feet were still sticking up out of the water because he could feel the wind blowing across them. He imagined them finding him like that, could picture everyone he knew standing at the rim of the pit, looking down at his feet sticking out of the water and crying. Harry tried breathing in some of the dark water, hoping to make his end as quick as possible, but as soon as he tasted the dirt-like bitterness he scrambled to turn himself around and brought his head out, choking and gagging.

Harry lay and rested while he caught his breath. His nearness to death had calmed him, and he felt better able to think, but the cramps came back and he felt himself getting weaker. He thought of his last summer, sitting on the back porch, watching the heat shimmering over the highway and the flat field beyond. "Don't stay out there in the heat too long," his mother said from the other side of the screen door. "Why don't you come inside where it's cooler?"

"Devil," Harry said, in as loud and calm a voice as he could muster. "Devil, if Jesus won't help me maybe you will. All I want to do is get out of here. Please help me. Please." He waited with his eyes closed, listening for a voice, waiting for an acknowledgment. He opened his eyes and looked up, but all he saw was the angry sky, threatening rain.

Too tired to cry or curse, he lay there in the water, awaiting death. After awhile it started to rain. He turned over, letting the warm drops splash on his face. It was then that he saw the road, looking like a slash of mud on the gray-brown gravel. Directly across the pit from him was the remnant of the road that trucks had used to haul gravel out of the pit. The lower part of the road had caved in, so that when the water level was low you didn't even notice that the road was there, but with the water so high, the road came down almost to the surface. Harry blinked, hoping that the road wouldn't disappear when he opened his eyes. It was still there, and he began scuttling around the edge of the pit, not trusting himself to swim straight across.

He ran all the way home in warm, heavy rain. It fell so fast and so hard that it stood in the street, giving him the feeling that he was running on water.

He met his brother a few doors away from home, walking toward him with his head down, wearing their father's yellow slicker suit and hat. Jake looked up as Harry ran towards him.

"Where have you been, you dummy? Dad sent me out to look for you. You're really in trouble now, you know it? Hey, what's the matter with you?"

Harry ran past him and on to his house. He ran up the steps and plunged through the door and stood dripping and panting in the dark hallway. The face of Satan seemed burned into his vision. He saw it in the pattern of the wallpaper, in the painting of a vase of flowers at the opposite end of the hall. He switched on the light and the faces disappeared, and he found that he was cold and incredibly tired.

"Harry? Is that you?" his father asked. "Jake? Did you find him?"

Harry stood, shivering, not daring to answer but afraid also of not answering. He heard his father put down the newspaper and walk slowly towards the hall, his stockinged feet swishing softly on the wood floor.

Harry didn't look up, not even when he saw his father's shadow at his feet, knowing his father's head was almost at the light fixture, feeling the light and the heat from the bulb being blocked out by his father's size.

"What's the matter, son? Where's your brother? Where have you been?"

"He's coming," was all that Harry could manage, then he ran around his father and through the living room, into the other hallway to the room he shared with Jake. He sat down heavily on the bottom bunk, and the full weight of what he had done came to him. But he couldn't cry. Whatever deal he had made with the devil was better than death. He thought of the feel and the smell of the cold, heavy water in his nose and throat, and his chest ached again and he felt himself stiffen all over. Whatever the devil came and asked him to do would be better than lying cold and dead at the bottom of the dark, murky pit.

THE BLUE UNIFORM

by

F.N. WRIGHT

This is the story of my career with the United States Postal Service. You have to understand, it was a time of desperation for me. My wardrobe of T-shirts and levis had become spattered with grease and tattered with holes; my field jacket had seen better days. I needed some new stuff, you know. But nobody I knew ever actually *paid* for clothes.

I was complaining about my situation to my letter carrier one day when he delivered my welfare check—a check I was receiving monthly by fraudulent means. Anyway, he mentioned that the USPS gave all their letter carriers a uniform allowance. That's when I noticed how downtown his blue uniform looked.

For as long as I could remember uniforms had attracted chicks. Well, except for that time when we were involved in Nam, when a chick might spit in your face and call you a baby-killer if you were in uniform.

But that was a long time ago, and the chicks I was after hadn't even been born yet. I knew if I had a letter carrier uniform the worst thing that might happen to me was to be mistaken for a bus driver.

That made something click in my head. I would be styling behind the wheel of my psychedelic painted school bus dressed in a downtown-looking uniform like that.

By this time me and my letter carrier are two miles from my house. He's like running, and before I'm totally dead out of breath, I ask him if he'll sell me one of his uniforms.

He puffed out his chest and told me it would be sacrilegious to sell one of his uniforms. Even worn out, he said they were still government property. Said he was a 204b—that's a supervisor in training—and that he was going to keep all of his uniforms lined up neatly in his closet when he became a real supervisor so he'd remember what it'd been like under fire when he was no longer one of the troops.

My head was spinning by then. Running with him for two miles listening to his gibberish had made me tired, and I needed a nap. The nearest park bench was too far away, so I collapsed on the lawn of his next delivery while he ran up to the mailbox.

Next thing I know he was yelling, "Look at this card! This customer doesn't want you walking on his grass!"

I opened one eye and saw him waving this yellow card in my face. I said look, man, it's obvious I'm not walking on the grass. I'm flat-assed out on my fucking back, and you're blocking my sun.

I rolled onto my side and watched him run to the next house through my one open eye. He destroyed a well-tended flower garden in his hurry to reach the mailbox.

I was not impressed. You shouldn't run through other people's flower gardens with your ass sitting on your shoulders like that.

But I was still impressed with his blue uniform.

*   *   *

It took me over a year to get hired by the USPS. While I was waiting I repainted my school bus. When I was finished it looked like a psychedelic postal vehicle. I definitely needed one of those uniforms now.

Then I learned that I wouldn't get my clothing allowance until I'd passed a 90-day probationary period. And I was told that the slightest vehicular-type accident meant immediate termination.

Soon I was adding to my vocabulary. I'd *route flats* on a *B.B.*, sidestep crazed clerks pushing *BMC*s, try not to get caught *deviating*, and ask for a *3996* every day. Then I'd argue with a supervisor or 204b about whether the route I was carrying was an 8-hour route or not.

I have to tell you, there wasn't an 8-hour route in the office. They were more like 12-hour routes. The city had more than doubled in size during the past ten years and there hadn't been one adjustment made during that time. I drove like a madman to meet the times the supervisors were allowing me to do my deliveries in. They stressed safety, but the last thing they did was give me enough time to perform my work safely.

I have to tell you about the insane logic I faced every day. One day, while waiting for my uniform allowance, a supervisor noticed I was wearing my old jungle boots. He sent me home, saying they were unsafe for the workroom floor because they didn't have leather uppers.

I wondered, as I took the rest of the day off to find suitable footwear, why the government hadn't realized how unsafe those boots were to wear when they sent me to Nam in them.

Supervisors and 204b's, especially 204b's, never made much sense. Some days these 204b's are letter carriers and other days they play like supervisors. They leave their blue uniform hanging in the closet and report to work in a necktie or dress and a handful of pens and pencils to shuffle reams of government paperwork around and to screw with their fellow letter carriers' heads.

I understood their confusion. Neckties actually worn around the neck cut off the flow of blood to your brain. Ya gotta understand, I'm not against neckties, as long as they are worn and used properly. There are five neckties in my wardrobe. One I use for a headband, and the other four to tie chicks to my bedposts.

I am sounding like a deviant as I deviate from my story about the blue uniform. I must get back on the right track now. The USPS teaches us not to deviate.

In spite of two minor vehicular accidents I made it through the 90-day probationary period. My first accident was when I knocked off a mirror on one of the jeeps I was driving when I hit a mailbox with it. I did not panic. I disconnected the odometer (they actually record your daily mileage), deviated from my route, and replaced the broken mirror with one from my psychedelic postal-looking school bus. It stuck out like a Sissy Hankshaw thumb, but no one in management noticed because there wasn't any blood reaching their brains.

The second accident was a little more complicated, but just as minor. I was distracted by a 15 year-old chick in shorts and scraped some paint off the front bumper. I couldn't deviate to my pad to touch up the damage because all my paint is day-glo psychedelic.

I was wondering what I was going to do as I drove to the next part of the route. It was a *park and loop* instead of *mounted*. Someone had just watered their lawn, and the answer came to me when I got out of the jeep and stepped into some mud. I dabbed mud on the bumper, knowing that when it dried it would cover the slight scrape the 15 year-old chick had caused.

So yes, I made it through probation, but it was not easy. I really did not speed through it, man. Running is not my style. I was actually so slow that I'm surprised they kept me. I think it was because there was a "hiring freeze" in effect and they were keeping anyone who didn't have, or wasn't, a wreck.

Now picture this: I'm returning to the post office after carrying *swings* for fellow letter carriers. The supervisor will be surprised, because it is not dark yet. I did not take my usual hour siesta because I knew a uniform salesman was going to be there.

And there he is. He has set up shop near the carrier entrance. I cannot wait to punch out. I must shop for my blue uniform.

Now I'm standing there with the salesman, and I am overwhelmed by his selection. And I am confused. These uniforms are expensive, and my clothing allotment is a little under $200. I must be selective and shop carefully.

The clothing salesman is getting impatient, but I remain cool. I do not let him rush me like supervisors and 204b's have tried to do for three months. As the sun goes down, I make up my mind.

I choose two of those new Safari shirts you don't have to tuck in. Wow, they are just like shirts barbers and pharmacists wear, but they are cool blue instead of white.

Shorts! I have to have a pair of those long-legged shorts, and those socks that come all the way up to the knees. Yes, and a Sam Brown belt to attach my *arrow key* to.

No, I do not want a baseball cap, man. Just watching an athletic event exhausts me. But I must have a pith helmet and one of those bus driver caps.

Oh man, dig this. Look at all these pins. They are replicas of stamps. I must have one of each and a pair of those hiking boots with soft leather uppers.

No—forget the boots. I'll stick to the steel-toed construction worker boots I've been wearing in lieu of my unsafe jungle boots. You never know when you might drop a letter on your toes.

The uniform salesman is telling me I have to pay cash for the pins. The news does not bother me. I have not had to cash one of my fraudulent welfare checks since I started work for the USPS. I can afford all of them.

I must add one more thing to my uniform: I have to have one of those jackets with the patch over the left breast pocket that proudly proclaims:

LETTER CARRIER. No one will mistake me for a bus driver when they see that.

A few days later my uniform arrives. My supervisor for the day has just given it to me, and I feel hyper-ventilation coming on like a seaweed high rush. I must take emergency annual leave so I can go to my pad and affix my postage stamp pins to my downtown blue uniform.

I have so many pins that I have to put some of them on my shirts, but that's cool. It means more of them to show off when I remove my jacket.

It is the next morning, and I'm walking towards my postal-looking psychedelic painted school bus. I am tired, because I spent the night standing at attention and admiring my blue uniform in my full-length mirror.

It's cool. My pace is proud and brisk, and I have hidden my patriotic eyes behind my girl-watcher shades. My supervisor will never know how tired I am and think he needs to contact *EAP* to rehabilitate me because he might look into my eyes and think I was up all night smoking seaweed.

My pith helmet is pulled low over my shades, held securely in place by the chin strap. I am wearing high socks and my groovy, long-legged shorts held up by my Sam Brown belt. Only my knees will be exposed to the sun. My safari shirt hangs below the bottom of my jacket, which adds more class to my cool appearance. I am carrying my bus driver hat so I can change headwear throughout the day.

I am at work, sitting in the breakroom with two cups of coffee. I must get a caffeine high going before it's time to clock in. I'm still hiding behind my girl-watcher shades, and I cannot help but notice how I stand out. Guys and gals I've been working with for three months don't recognize me, seeing me in uniform for the first time. Their uniforms aren't as hip-looking as mine. Yes, I shopped wisely. I must remember to tell the supervisors I can no longer carry walking routes. A satchel might scratch my pins.

What's this shit? The breakroom is being invaded by neckties, dresses and skirts. I remember now: they are training an army of 204b's today. It is, like, frightening. It is like being of the land and seeing the sky darken with locusts.

A fuzz-faced necktie walks over and lightly punches me on the shoulder. He is speaking gibberish to me. "You look RARING to go!" he says in a voice light years from puberty. "I like to wake up to the sight of a fired-up carrier in the morning! Run your route today, troop!"

I am speechless. I must leave before I puke all over his spit-shined shoes.

* * *

The phone is ringing. It is ringing off the hook, but I can't find its muffled sound in the clutter. It rings incessantly for a week before I find it buried under the moldy, muck-infested dishes in my sink. Or is it my easy chair? It doesn't matter because I have found the phone.

It is one of the supervisors from work. He is telling me I'm AWOL. I tell him Man, I haven't heard that term since my army days. AWOL? He lightens up a little and tells me it isn't as serious as being AWOL from the military, but that it is serious.

Now he's asking me when I'm coming back. I have never saved up so much money in my life, so I tell him I don't know. Maybe when my savings run out.

I have made him angry. The Postmaster General of the United States will not like my attitude. I tell him that the last Postmaster that had his shit together was the first one, and that he would've understood me. He doesn't know who I'm talking about. He has so much daylight passing through his ears that he doesn't know a thing about life away from the job. I have to hang up the phone.

It seems serious. I may have the F.B.I. at the door for being AWOL from the USPS. They won't come after me until I am officially a deserter. I have 30 days before they can change my status. I will take 29 days off to think about everything, and if I decide to report back I will tell them I was sick instead of AWOL. I will tell them I have been diagnosed with Postal Brain Rot. I'd better take two aspirins and get some rest before I do anything else.

OLD TIMES

by

ALBERT NOUS

I was born in Albany, New York, on August 12, 1910. It was the year of the five-cent beer, twenty-five-cent dinner, fifty-cent haircut and twenty-five cent shave from the barber, Tony, who was my father. He was born Ontonio Azar in 1888 in Beirut, Lebanon. He came to the United States when he was nine.

He had a barber shop on Green Street, two doors down from Killips Laundry and Keeler's Restaurant. Mr. Keeler was my Dad's best customer and thought nothing of tipping a dollar.

My dad was small, all of 5 feet 2 inches, but he had a heart as large as heaven. He survived his younger years pushing a cart around New York City peddling thread, needles and linens for the ladies that lived in the tenement houses on 8th Avenue. It was a way of making a living—the hard way—but it was honest work in spite of the long hours pushing and sweating in the summer and standing the cold days of winter. He came in contact with all types of people and treated all with respect and compassion. Sometimes he was so exhausted at the end of a day he would fall asleep at the supper table.

In 1905 my dad and grandmother moved to Albany. In 1907 he began attending a barber school. After two years of working for fifty cents a day as an apprentice barber he finally opened his one-chair shop on Green Street.

That same year my father became a U.S. citizen and married my mother, Sadie Arsoury. It was an arranged marriage; my mother was only thirteen at the time, and they had never met before. Nine years later they were divorced, but on Sundays Mother would still visit to cook, console, and show that she cared for all of us, even my father. But when she remarried, my sister Sarah, my two brothers Joseph and Victor and myself were put into St. Coleman's Home in Watervliet. It was a temporary solution, because my father had trouble caring for all of us. The sisters and priests at the orphanage instilled in our hearts and minds a deep love for God and His wonderous works.

Within a year my dad took us out of the orphanage and we settled in Troy. It was a five-dollar a month basement flat with a one-chair barber shop. We lived in three rooms in the rear of the shop, but we were all together again. My dad's love, patience and fortitude gave our family a sense of togetherness.

Many times we waited for him to make fifty cents so we could go and buy a can of beans and some bologna and bread. We lived on butter, Campbell's beans, bologna, bread and coffee. My father was a great one for beans and macaroni—we would have it three or four times a week. Once in a while we would have a treat and he would add hot dogs to it. Only through the kindness of Mr. O'Brien, who ran a grocery store on the corner of 8th & Middleburg, and Joe Harbour, who had a meat market on 9th & Middleburg, did we survive the lean years of the Depression.

Mrs. Hurley had a store on Middleburg and 9th streets, across from the meat market, where we bought our ice cream cones. Adjacent to the store were stone steps leading into the apartments upstairs. If we got noisy or to fooling around Mrs. Hurley would get a bucket of water and wet down the stone steps. You had to be alert or else you got a wet bottom.

Discipline by my dad was a barber's strap on my bottom and being sent to bed without supper. Who cared anyway—I was getting tired of beans and macaroni. But he was a forgiving father, and the next day he would give me a haircut and a ten-cent piece for a soda.

My father ran a clean barber shop. He was a union member and every month I had to pay his dues to Mr. Walsh, who had a barber shop next door to Vedder's Variety Store on the corner of River Street and Ingalls Avenue. I tried learning the barber trade. My first job was lathering up the beards of the customers. Sometimes I got soap in their mouths, but my dad would tell them I was just learning. That lasted until I started learning to use the razor. My first shaving customer ran from the barber shop with my dad's barber cloth flapping in the wind. We never saw him again, and that ended my career as a barber.

School One, which we attended, was directed by Mr. Lisle. I remember very well the two-foot ruler he kept in his desk drawer in his office. One day I dipped the braid of the girl in front of me in my inkwell. Boy did I get it from Mr. Lisle's ruler, as well as getting booted in my rear from the girl's father outside of the school building. After that I became such a teacher's pet that she let me clean the blackboard erasers outside in the school alley.

I remember walking to school with my books under my arms and my bookstrap holding up my trousers. The kids wore knickers with a strap at the knees. If you had holes in your pockets and played marbles the marbles would go through the holes and bunch up at your knees. Everything went in the hole: your pennies, your gum, your caramels. That night you would tie up the hole with a string. Have you ever tried running with a knicker full of apples? Duncan's farm had a huge apple orchard on North Lake Avenue where the Frear Park Golf Course is now. The grapes were luscious, too—but don't trip and fall with your knickers full of them. I did, and was the only kid in the world with blue legs and knees. Of course I got a licking from my dad, but who cares. The grapes were very tasty.

Mrs. Adams had the candy store across from School One. It was one of the first stops after school. For five cents you got two maple candies, six Mary Janes and three caramels. From there we went home and changed into old knock-about clothes and looked for some sort of mischief to get into.

Sometimes we would go skinny-dipping in the first reservoir off Oakwood Avenue. Other times we swam in the Hudson River off Middleburg Street and would hitch a ride on the river barges and get chased off by the crew of the tugboat. We would watch a man in a boat at the foot of Ingalls Avenue who would ferry Ford workers across the river to the Ford plant for five cents each. At 7 a.m. and 4 p.m. he was always ready for his passengers, and people would wave to him from the river banks. Between ferrying the workers he would ride near the dam and fish for carp, eels and other fish, catching them in his net at the end of the boat and selling them to the local fish markets. At that time river pollution was unheard of. Other times we would walk to the foot of Broadway in Troy and watch "The Trojan" passenger boat turn around in the river and head for New York City. One day my dad took us to Midway Beach and we marveled at the smoothness of the boat. On my first roller coaster ride I lost a pack of gum, seven pennies, and my stomach. On the beach the ladies would breast-feed their crying babies.

Sometimes when coming home from School One I would watch Mr. Cassidy shoe horses in a building where Shelftel Glass Company is now. It was an old barn with stalls. How that Mr. Cassidy, as short as he was, could handle the big horses hoofs I'll never know.

Later I would watch the firemen at the firehouse on North and River Streets. When an alarm sounded the horses would come out of the stalls and back up to the fire engine without a word from the firemen. Then the harnesses would come down and the firemen would complete harnessing them. They would then race out of the firehouse with smoke pouring out of the boiler in the back end of the fire engine, which was stoked with coal by a fireman to keep the pressure up to pump water out of the fire hydrants.

Sometimes we would water the elephants in Laurete Park at Glen Avenue and River Street. The circus men would give you a free pass if you carried 100 buckets of water to the elephants. The circus was exciting but after carrying the buckets I would be so tired that I would fall asleep during the intermission way up in the top benches where the Clyde Brothers circus men would put all the workers. What a feeling to wake up and find everyone gone.

Then came the long trolley car ride home with all the kids falling asleep. The motorman would wake us up at the end of the line. There was a trolley car line on Oakwood Avenue that terminated at St. Peter's Cemetery. The motorman would pull the rear cow catcher up and lower the front one and proceed back to downtown Troy. The United Traction Company had the trolley car barn at 12th and Second Avenue. In summer they had open-air trolley cars, and in warm weather you got a cool ride down Second Avenue. They had rolled curtains on the sides in case of rain, with a motorman in front and a conductor to collect the ten-cent fare. It was a thrill to ride to Congress Street—everyone saw you and sometimes you yelled at kids you knew.

The happiest times of my childhood were the days spent at the Troy Boy's Club. The club was under the direction of Mr. Edward Kane. He was a gentle, kind and patient man whom all the kids respected. Roy Filkins had a harmonica band at the club. He was also a desk clerk at the YMCA on First Street.

At one time we used to go to the Palace Theater on Hoosick and Fifth Avenue. They would give food baskets as door prizes. The first time I won I brought the basket of groceries home. My dad thought I had stolen it, but my brother, Joe, told him what had happened. From then on I always got money to go to the movies at the Palace on grocery giveaway nights. After the movies we would go to John Tatakis Store on North Street and Sixth Avenue and get a five-cent soda. All it had was a little chocolate syrup and carbonated water, which was then stirred like mad.

Sometimes on Sunday we would all dress up in our good clothes and visit the Perris's and Betars who then lived on Hamilton Avenue. My dad knew how to play the mandolin, and with a shot of anisette along side and a table loaded with all kinds of Syrian dishes everyone had a high old-fashioned get-together.

During the cold winter months we had one kitchen stove to keep us warm, even though the fire grates were held up by bricks. It was a nightly event to sit around the stove and cook chestnuts. Sometimes we would discuss what we were going to be when we got older. Sometimes we ran out of coal for the stove and would walk along the railroad tracks picking up lumps of soft coal to take home.

We would ride our sleighs from the top of Middleburg Street down the hill across the railroad tracks to Sixth Avenue. Some families living on Oakwood Avenue built toboggans that could hold 12 people, with a steering wheel in front and a brake in the back to stop the toboggan when it got to Hoosick Street. In those days there were few cars; some kids would act as guards at street corners to let the toboggans pass.

We looked forward to a warm school. Sometimes we would have nothing to eat during lunch period, but the neighbors, like Mrs. Robinson, would put extra sandwiches in her son's lunch box to give to the Nous boys. Sometimes my brothers and I would have supper at the Robinson's home. It was a feast as far as we were concerned: heaping bowls of beef stew and lots of homebaked bread and uncolored margarine. Being hungry kids, we ate and asked God to bless the whole Robinson household.

One favorite stop was Keller's Bakery, where you got cookies for one cent a piece, three sugar buns for eight cents and butternut bread for seven cents a loaf. Stubblebean and Johnny Bejian served you. Mr. Keller always gave bread and other baked goods free to the poor in the neighborhood. Many a supper I had with day-old bread with sugar sprinkled on top. We would dig in, but not before we had a show of hands for inspection. In those days no one was concerned about their hearts or dieting. It was good, nourishing food that satisfied a growing kid's hunger. Our next door neighbor, Mr. Gervisio, would give us all their bruised vegetables. My dad would make a salad, adding oil and vinegar and placing it in the center of the table with Keller's butternut bread.

Each day the farmer would come around with cans of whole milk and a big quart ladle. They got five cents for a quart of milk in your own pail—a new pail was 20 cents extra. Often milk pails would double as a beer pail. At Mr. O'Brien's bar working men got free soup and lunch when they bought a beer. Mr. O'Brien the saloon owner would let me have a sandwich once in a while. After the farmer the ragman would come around with his wagon and tired old horse. He would yell "Any rags, any bones, any bottles today?". We kids got five cents for a pound of rags and a penny for a bottle.

Lifestyles in those days seemed less hectic, more relaxed and with an awareness that everyone cared about each other's problems. On warm summer nights families would sit on the front porch and steps of their homes and talk and laugh about the events of the day. Afterward came cookies and lemonade to enjoy on those balmy evenings. One family would make the eligible daughter put on a pretty dress, and boy oh boy she sure was a good looker. I used to pass her house every night just to get a look at her. My dream burst when they moved away to Vermont. When you're young, love could be turned off and on like a faucet, so everyday was a new beginning for romance.

The first house party I went to was on River Street. Somehow the fun began by playing Post Office. I remember the father of the girl having the party was always the doorman and you could only spend two minutes kissing the girl. If you did not come out in two minutes, a big hairy arm would reach in and grab you by the seat of your pants, so you made sure your trousers were up and belted. At 10 p.m. the hairy arm would pull out a railroad watch and bellow "the party's over!"

Mothers and fathers would hold birthday parties for their kids. All the kids would be in the parlor and the old folks would stay in the kitchen or back yard, depending on the weather. One parent I knew made his sons fetch a pail of beer at the local saloon. Before the party was over a lot of pails of beer changed hands. Some of the elderly ladies loved to quaff down a beer or two, but they did it where no one could see them — drinking down the suds and loving every minute of it. We kids didn't care—we were playing post office in the bedroom off the parlor. Then came the goodies, like homemade baked beans, potato salad, homemade bread and, best of all, Wager Brothers Birch Beer.

As a boy of 15 I used to do odd jobs to make money, even helping a bootlegger make bathtub gin. I would fill pint bottles and cork them, delivering them for seventy-five cents a pint. Fifty cents went to the bootlegger and twenty-five cents to me for the delivery. A lot of the older crowd had flasks which they carried on their hips when they went to a party or dance. When they got drunk the host or hostess would put them in bed until they sobered up.

Mr. and Mrs. Stacy were loveable people who cooked dinner every Saturday night at the YMCA. A complete meal was served at 8 p.m. for $1.25. Then we danced at the YWCA where they had more chaperons than any other dance hall. If you danced too close with your partner they would come over to tell you about it. At 11 p.m. the dance was over and the chaperons walked all the men out the front door. No sneaking a hug or kiss. A date in those days consisted of a movie and afterwards a soda at Knowlsons, Fazolis or Mancenellis. Your date had to be home by 10 p.m. Sometimes her mother or father would meet the bus to see that their precious daughter got home safely. You got no kiss goodbye, just a squeeze of the hand. The entire evening cost $2.50 including gum and bus fare.

On Sundays you could rent a horse and buggy for two dollars a day at Lindy's Stables on the Congress Street tunnel or at Mose's Livery in the alley just off Rennselaer Street. Those poor horses were so thin. When I went into the country I would let the horse gorge itself on fresh grass. Sometimes my dates would tell me I thought more of the horses than I did of them. Being a curly headed, goodlooking kid, I soon found out who came first.

I got a job after school as a soda fountain attendant at the Mayflower Sweete Shoppe on River Street near Millcahys Furniture Store. I took and made up orders for sundaes, banana splits, frosts, and malted milks—any flavor. Mr. George Cholakis was my boss. After a few errors and spills I became quite a good soda jerk. I made the Romeo and Juliet sundae, Adam and Eve in a banana boat, strawberry and chocolate marshmallow sundaes, and, last but not least, a King Tut sundae. Mr. Cholakis always served real whipped cream on all his ice cream and even made up fruits and homemade chocolate candies. At the end of my day I would mix malt, heavy cream, ice cream and an egg, beat the life out of it and drink it. There was a nickleodeon in the rear of the shoppe. It contained a violin that only played an old-time melody, "Humoresque." I must have heard that tune about 3000 hours and could count every note in the music. Then I got laid off and returned to depression times.

I finally jot a job at the A&P Grocery Store on 6th Avenue and worked with the store's manager, Mr. Connally. My job was to keep the coffee bins full of coffee beans, which came in huge bags. I would then grind the coffee beans. It had a big wheel which I turned to give the customer a choice of how they wanted their coffee ground. I also kept the grocery shelves filled with canned goods. I did all this for fifty cents an hour, but it was a job. I made five dollars a day, and would give my dad three dollars and keep two. Sometimes I went overboard and spent two dollars on a pair of used knicker trousers so I could have a warm pair to wear. Often we went to bed with our stockings and trousers on because during the night the kitchen stove would go out and it got very cold in the apartment.

Troy Buick sold new cars for $1,000. A new Plymouth Roadster went for $750 at Filson Auto. At that time I owned a car I called "Moon". It had a cone clutch and sometimes you had to put Fuller's Earth in a hole at the top to make the car move. I got rid of that car and bought a 1927 Ford Touring car for $10. That same night I brought my car to a gal friend to show her and had to leave it there because the headlights wouldn't work. I walked from Cohoes to Troy that night. So there I was with no gal, no car, and no dime for car fare.

The car had no top, and Lord help you if you got caught in a rainstorm. The front floorboards were also rotted out. One night I had a date and she had to ride with her legs up on the seat. Then it started to rain. If we had been ducks we would have felt right at home. But my five dollar pair of trousers shrunk up so much that after I dropped my date off at her house I went up the alley, removed them, and rode home in my underwear. Thank God I had longjohns on.

The churches in Troy were always so crowded on Sundays that the cops directed traffic at all the church masses. St. Peter's Church had the busiest parish. St. Patrick's Church was then run by Father Merns. I remember delivering the sacramental wine in a 55 gallon barrel which we slid down a wooden ramp into the basement of the church. He ruled his church and parish but was kind, fair and generous.

Being the oldest, it was my responsibility each month to pick up a $12 welfare check from the Welfare Commissioner, Mr. Nora Burke. This fed a family of five and bought a quarter ton of coal to keep us warm.

Some parents were too proud to accept the money, but that pride went out the window when your children went hungry.

People cared about each other and shared all their trials and tribulations. Neighbors cared about neighbors. In times of sorrow the children of the bereaved were cared for by neighbors, who donated food. In those days the undertaker would put a black flowered wreath on the front door of a home to show folks where the deceased was laid out, usually in the front parlor. All the donated food was put on the kitchen table for the sorrow-stricken family to enjoy. Somehow I believe that a part of all the love and joys shared by the deceased went with them to the hereafter.

I'll never forget the mother of a beautiful girl that had developed tuberculosis when she was 9 years old. The mother could not bear to see her daughter placed in Marshall's Sanitarium in Wynanskill, choosing to take care of her at home. During the summer months she would dress her up in a pinafore dress with long white stockings and low-cut shoes. She would seat her in her favorite chair on the front porch so she could see and talk to her school chums that she missed so much. Sometimes I would sit with her and discuss world events and the beautiful people in her life. She always had her Raggedy Ann doll with her whether sitting on the front porch or going to bed. She often told me that the nights were so long because all she could do was cough and cough up phlegm in a sputum cup, which her mother kept on a stand near her bed. During the night she often heard her mother sobbing in her bedroom. Sometimes the parents and the daughter would pray together in the parlor hoping for a miracle, but both parents knew it was up to God and his angels. At the stroke of 6:00 a.m. on a day in January in 1920 the Good Lord needed more angels in heaven and took all the little girl's pain and hurt away forever, giving her eternal joy and peace. I cried when they buried her in St. Peter's Cemetery and watched from a hilltop as they lowered her into the grave. Somehow I felt God was with me watching.

SALOON

by

Frank Criscenti

"My boyfriend kicked me out," she says.

The .22 automatic shifts in the pocket of my leather jacket.

"The Saloon is the oldest continuously-operated barroom in San Francisco," Steve says.

My .22 automatic is a handsome weapon. Gleaming, silvered steel, a sleek, compact, handful of pop. A demon killer. Slayer of all that is evil.

The band, "Fenders from Hell", sets up their instruments.

I'm here, depressed. It's my friend Toby's last night in the City. In the hot bar my pistol feels air-conditioned cool to the touch.

The three of us sit next to the woman whose boyfriend dumped her. She lights up a smoke, her second since we arrived just minutes ago. "I have a toothache," she says. She looks it. She's wearing a pin-striped, businesswoman's coat and skirt with bright white tennis shoes. Her face was pretty once, before the cigarettes and scotch. Her clothing hangs without pretense.

Twang. The instruments speak with amplified curses.

Hippies at the bar.

Two hundred year old fat woman in Spandex pants, silk-shirt made from big spiders—according to the drunk hippie at the bar. Pure silk shirt open to her navel. The kind of woman a sober man won't look at. Butch haircut, peroxide blonde, spiked bracelet.

Is Elvis alive?

My pistol's alive, but life is critically ill. All I'd known—collapsing in a bar that's operated since 1862, according to Steve. I have no reason to disbelieve Steve. I believe anyone, anywhere.

The band wanted to. I could feel it building. They wanted to do what bands do. Twang. Twang.

They're off.

Suburban-dressed chubby woman smiles gratefully at the guitar-wielding boys. She nods. Her pelvis catches. She's dancing. "You play it. I'll do it."

There's a beautiful woman in a tight, black, shoulder-sliding dress sitting next to me. I won't look at her because I don't want her to know how beautiful I think she is. I couldn't take that—her knowing.

I'm getting old and changing. My life is falling in on itself, like a black hole sucking gravity. I breathe and inhale the world around me. Its noxious fumes and urine odors and barroom air from 1862. I was born in 1862.

I don't want the girl in the black dress to see how I've changed. I stare at her while she dances. Her breasts slide under the fabric. Her hips thrust against the atmosphere. The women I stare at no longer stare back.

The band flies. The noise screams in my ears.

There is a woman in a tie-dye t-shirt pounding the floor with blue-suede bitch boots, no lie. Her mini-skirt hikes up around her beautiful legs and her thighs sweat. She grabs her hips and humps at the band. Her fingers point. Spit flecks at the side of her mouth. Steve says she's on blotter acid.

Her friend looks like a Munchkin. An ageless, sexless, short fat Wayne Newton look-alike who might really be a woman for all I know. I've lost track of what women can do to look like men.

Toby's found a woman at the bar.

The waitress grabs my bobbing head and pushes it toward the table so I won't spill her drinks. This is my life at thirty-seven. A woman pinning my head to the table so she won't spill her drinks. This is my outlook. My eyes focus on a moist ring from a bottle of beer. In this ring are all the elements necessary to life. I lick the ring and order more beers.

There's an old man standing drunk in front of the bandstand. He seems to be contemplating these screeching, frantic sounds. The whole bar is going insane and this skinny, white-haired, pot-bellied lecher is hearing jazz where there is no jazz to hear. He's feeling sorry for himself because the young girls he asks to dance just walk away from him.

I'm feeling sorry for myself, no doubt.

The insanity continues all around me.

My wife said it earlier today. "If you want out, I want out."

There it was, sounding like "What'll you have" from a bartender. "A beer and an estrangement please." Ten years of footprints on each other's hearts, gone in something as unpoetic and pathetic as that. "If you do, I do."

Now another Thursday night out with the boys. I finger the small gun and know what I've got to do.

The band decides on a break.

The Saloon is shoulder to shoulder with people. I'm separated from the woman with the toothache. I keep my back to the beautiful girl. Toby is back from the bar and moving in on another girl who has crowded in at our table with the couple she came with.

"I've published two articles in women's magazines," she says.

I think of my story in the mail, waiting to be rejected by a women's magazine.

"I'd kill for that," I say, stroking the barrel of the toy in my pocket. She smiles.

The band cranks up again. She and Toby take to the dance floor. I knock my beer off the table and it falls into my hand as if by magic.

I watch some little Japanese bar creature dancing with three girls, all facing the same direction.

I see a Chinese girl with a razor smile. She's counting the change rattling in her boyfriend's pocket. She's a matron before her time.

The Arabs are at the bar.

The hippies are wearing bermuda shorts.

Tie-dye's skirt is folded up around her ass. She is totally immersed in the slash of sounds. Ten thousand hits of blotter acid chase each other around her brain.

I get up, kneel down, and lick where her sweat has dripped on the splintered floor. Then I try to lick her leg. The Munchkin kicks at me with his tiny feet. The bouncer deposits me in Fresno alley.

It's illegal to park on Fresno Alley. Verboten. Wrong. Morally reprehensible.

Some kid with an anguished haircut sticks his hands into the engine compartment of a recently deceased Volkswagen bug. Apparently his car has died in Fresno alley and there's no parking there.

I stagger up to him, feeling my gun.

He curses: "Goddamsonofabitchmotherfuckingbastardfucking car."

First I feel sympathy. Then I feel anger.

No parking.

"What's wrong?" I ask.

"Fucker died on me," he says.

"You can't park here."

"What?" He looks up from the back of the bug.

"I said you can't park here. No parking."

"Fuck you." He sticks his face back under the hood.

I pull the gun out. It shines in the moonlight. I look into the barrel of it. I can hear the band inside The Saloon. I think about it, just for a second.

"You can't park here," I repeat, without knowing why.

The kid looks up from the rear of the car again. His face is overflowing with malice. "Get the fuck . . . " He notices the gun in my hand.

I point it at him, because guns are supposed to point.

He runs.

I go around to the back of his car. Poor car. It's hoses are broken. It's wires are crossed. I pump several shots into the engine and walk off down the alleyway.

A SECRET PLACE

by

S.J. Rayner

It was a dismal morning—cold and grey. His chest ached; breathing came hard. Fear and despair made it almost impossible for him to move. Forcing his legs forward, he boarded the bus and sat stiffly, the valise between his legs. He was off to fight a war he knew or cared nothing about.

He closed his eyes and pictured his father standing on the bus platform, smiling bravely. He knew that smile. He saw it often enough when he was sick. His mother: she could never hide her feelings. The handkerchief she waved would be wet with tears. That was why he sometimes hated her—his father, too; they were so stupidly sentimental. But he had no complaints. They had sheltered and protected him these eighteen years. Now he was alone.

The bus lurched forward. An invisible thread snapped, separating him from his parents and the small town he had known all his life. His mouth went dry and a tear or two rolled along the edge of his eyelids. He held back; only little kids cried.

Hours later he pressed his face against the window as the bus rumbled across the George Washington Bridge. New York: Jammed-together buildings, jammed-in people, jammed-up traffic. "A haven of sin," his father preached. Frightened, yet strangely excited, he nervously bit his lower lip.

He stepped off the bus at the main terminal and walked the few blocks to Penn Station. As he walked past the buildings a young man winked and an old man begged. He shuddered, and tightened his grip on the valise: comb, toothbrush, toothpaste, underwear, pajamas, and a picture of his parents. All those things linked him with a peaceful, protected past. Even when some said he did bad things, like the time he took the neighbor's little girl to his room and took off her clothes.

Inside the station there were people milling everywhere—soldiers, loved ones, families, crowding in, pushing out, shouting, waving, laughing, crying. Somehow, it made him feel apart, alienated, like he was back home in the Grand Theater watching a newsreel.

He found a small space in the corner of the huge station and sat on the valise. Folding his arms across his stomach and holding his elbows, he tried to make himself as small and inconspicuous as possible. It was difficult; his tall, skinny frame stood out like a giant question mark.

Time passed slowly. The drone of voices competed with the hissing, chugging, rumbling sound of moving trains. He watched a soldier kissing his girl, and his mind wandered back to a brief summer romance at the seashore that ended with a stolen kiss. That kiss had stirred something deep inside him, something he had felt with the little neighbor girl. But the feeling with the girl on the beach was stronger—much stronger. If only she had not run off . . . . Sighing, his heart grew light. He was a soldier, or soon to be. Maybe he would find a girl to kiss good-bye, a girl who would not run away.

Doubt clouded his mind. He was stoop-shouldered and angled like an erector set. His hair was so light and fine that, from a distance, he appeared bald. Worse, dull brown eyes filled dark hollows in a gaunt face, while thin, bloodless lips stretched over sharp, crooked teeth. Still watching the soldier and his girl, he could not help thinking how ugly he was.

A hand touched his shoulder. Startled, he jumped to his feet.

"Hey, relax, honey. I'm not going to bite you." A slim girl of about twenty smiled at him. Thick mascara and heavy rouge gave her pretty face a painted-doll look. Even her blonde hair looked bleached. "You alone?" she asked.

"Y-y-yes," he stammered. He tried to keep his eyes on her face, but they kept drifting to the dress beneath her unbuttoned sweater. Though a drab, listless thing that looked like it had been through a hundred washings, it was the exposure that fascinated him. The light fabric traced every dip and curve of her shapely body while the V-shaped cleavage exposed half her breasts.

Her eyes were inviting as she said, "My name's Cybil. What's yours?"

The words tumbled from his mouth. "Claxton." He looked for her to laugh; everyone did.

She did not laugh. It was as if his name and what went with it were not funny at all.

"Where you heading, honey?"

He showed her his induction papers. "Fort Dix. I have to catch the three o'clock train."

She glanced at her watch. "Hmm. That gives you a good four hours to kill. Say, how would you like to spend some time in my flat? It ain't far from here."

Her voice was soft and soothing, like the purr of a kitten. He wanted to reach out and stroke her skin, see if it had the feel of fur; he resisted the impulse. Just like he resisted the idea of going with her. "Thanks anyway, Cybil, but I can't."

She tilted her head, squinting. "Can't? Everybody can . . . or most everybody. Are you one of them?"

He looked puzzled. "Them?"

She laughed. "Oh, I get it. Don't worry about a thing, honey. It's like taking candy from a baby." Gripping his arm, she tried to pull him along.

"Please, Cybil. Don't. I'll . . . I'll miss my train."

She giggled. "Fat chance. I'll have you back in plenty of time."

He looked around, embarrassed. He felt people were staring at them, mocking him. Her persistence only added to his embarrassment. He took a deep breath that seemed to compress his chest tighter than ever. "Whatever you say, Cybil." She squeezed his hand as they left Penn Station, the valise thumping lightly against his leg.

Some five blocks later they stopped in front of a large, rundown tenement sandwiched between two abandoned factories. He hesitated, debating whether to go back to the station or stick it out. She decided for him.

"It ain't exactly the Ritz, hon, but it's home," she winked. "Besides, it's as safe as if you were in your own bed. Cross my heart." Crossing herself, she let a finger linger on each nipple, raising small bumps in the thin dress. He stared at the bumps in surprise. One time not too long ago he found a picture of a naked woman in a trash pile. As in the picture, he thought female nipples were flat and lifeless, like those of the neighbor's little girl. He realized he was wrong; they actually had a life of their own, especially in grown-ups.

"Come on," she said, clutching his hand and leading him inside the darkened building. The smell of cabbage, garbage, and stale urine assailed his nostrils. He tried to hold his breath as they raced up the three flights to her flat, but to no avail. Gasping for air, he had not noticed a stocky, scar-faced man glaring at him from the shadows on the second landing.

Inside her flat he almost gagged. Garbage that had spilled on the floor was crawling with roaches. Clothing and stained bedclothes lay crumpled on the single bed. Dishes piled high on the sink were crusted with food. The stench of tobacco, liquor and perfume was everywhere.

She waved her arm in a wide arc. "Sorry about the mess, Claxton. I never did get a chance to tidy up." She clucked her tongue a few times and whistled. "Boy, you should have been here last night. It was wild— really wild."

He smiled weakly. "I don't mind . . . about the mess. He blushed. "I . . . I mean you should see our house sometimes," he lied. Actually, his mother always made sure their home had the look and smell of a well-scrubbed Dutch kitchen.

"I'll bet," she said, smiling. "Sit down. No. Not on the chair." She flung clothing and bedclothes on the floor. "On the bed. It's a lot more comfy."

He placed his valise next to the kitchen table and sat on the edge of the bed. He folded his hands between his legs.

"That's better, honey. You look cold. How about some wine?"

His face brightened. "Okay," he said, remembering the one time he drank a glass of wine. It was on his twelfth birthday. He was trying out a new pair of ice skates on the frozen pond behind his house when he broke through the ice. His father pulled him out of the frigid water and rushed him into the house. He stripped and dried him in front of the fireplace and wrapped him in a heavy woolen blanket. It did not help. He still shook and chattered like a crazy chipmunk.

Concerned, his father poured him a glass of sweet wine. He gulped it down, and almost at once he could sense a warm feeling spread through his body. It was like being sunburned on the inside, but much more pleasant. He experienced a nice, rosy glow that intensified when the family cat cuddled up to him. Excited, he stroked the soft fur harder and harder. When the cat cried in pain and attempted to pull away he accidently wrung her neck. He did not mean to. He hid the animal in a trunk containing his toys and buried the remains in the woods bordering the family property the next morning after his parents had left for work.

She stood before him holding two tumblers. A little of the wine spilled on her fingers as he grasped one of the glasses. "Sweets for the sweet," she said, slowly licking her fingers. "Know what I mean?"

He did not have the foggiest notion what she meant.

She finished her wine in one gulp. He did the same. His blood caught fire for an instant, then died out. There was no warm feeling inside, no urge to chuck his clothes; not that he would in front of the girl. There was not even a tiny bit of that nice, rosy glow that had excited him before. Disappointed, he stared somberly at the tumbler trying to divine what had gone wrong.

"Hey, don't look so down in the dumps. The fun's just starting." She slipped off her sweater and draped it over a chair. Turning her back to him, she added, "Unzip me, Claxton."

"Cybil! Quit your kidding."

"I'm not kidding. Now, be a good boy and give it a yank."

Blood rushed to his face; his heart pounded in his ears. He placed the glass on the floor and rubbed his shaky hands on his pants before fumbling with the zipper. After a few awkward tries, he got it unzipped, his fingers brushing against her skin. *It doesn't feel like fur*, he thought. *It's more like velvet.*

She shrugged her arms free of the dress and let it slip to the floor. Kicking off her shoes, she spun around saying, "You like, honey?"

He sat rigid. He was afraid to move or talk. Only his eyes were alive. They wandered freely, staring at her round, firm breasts and growth of lush black hair that pointed like an arrowhead to a secret place—a place he often dreamed of but never hoped to reach.

"Pussy got your tongue?"

He didn't answer.

"How much you got?" Cybil asked, her voice now crisp and business-like, her eyes no longer friendly. The sudden change in her attitude jolted him.

"I . . . I don't understand."

"Money, honey. Like my boyfriend always says, 'The best things in life ain't free.' "

He fumbled for his wallet and removed a ten-dollar bill—a gift from his father. He felt a twinge of conscience, but it quickly passed. Right now, his dad seemed a million miles away.

Smiling, she grabbed the money and shoved it into a dresser drawer. "Do you want me to undress you? Some guys like it that way."

Standing up, he averted his eyes. Close, she began unbuttoning his shirt. It was not long before he stood naked, his hands folded over his private parts.

With just a hint of a giggle, she flopped on the bed, spreading her legs wide. "Okay, baby. Time to skinny dip in the pool of love."

He stumbled forward and knelt between her legs, his knees pressing against her thighs. Then it happened—that nice, rosy glow. Only this time it was a thousand times stronger. . . .

He dressed slowly, experiencing an overwhelming sense of peace and contentment. When he made love to the girl, he had a different feeling; one of power, of loss of time and space, of his being bursting with energy and conveying the most thrilling sensations imaginable. Now, for the first time in his life, his chest did not ache and he could breathe much easier. More important, the world with its people-places, people-smells, people-things did not frighten him anymore. It was as if he suddenly realized everyone was just as vulnerable as him.

With great care he tucked the ten-dollar bill he had removed from the dresser into one of the plastic card holders in his wallet. From now on, it would be his lucky piece, his Open Sesame to strange and wonderful secret places all over the world. The army would see to that. He closed the door behind him and started down the stairway.

Beneath a dim bulb on the second landing he heard a door slam above him, followed by a hoarse, muffled cry and the sound of someone racing down the stairs. For a brief instant, he remembered the girl's remark about a boyfriend and felt his chest tighten. It was when he stared into the scarred, twisted face of a berserk man wielding a straight razor that he knew the mind-screeching terror the girl suffered as he had slowly strangled her.

Instinctively he raised the valise. The man kicked it, sending its contents flying. As the razor arched, Claxton felt as though he was falling through the ice.

LIVE OAK

by

GENE O'NEILL

The tree was old.

It had sprouted from an acorn on the West Coast about the same time Mary Easty was making her famous petition before the special court at Salem. As it grew the tree became a part of a green corridor that meandered the length of the coastal valley, a continuous grove of live oak growing along both sides of the river, providing cover for thirsty game and a plentiful drop of acorns which drew the attention of Wappo Indian hunters and gatherers. Later most of the oaken corridor and surrounding land were included in a grant from Mexico to General Mariano Guadlupe Vallejo, whose men cleared the land of both Indians and trees.

But the old oak remained, growing massive in a horizontal sense, its major branches reaching out instead of up, as if to claim all that it shaded. In addition to its exceptionally broad dimension there was something else curious about the tree's appearance: Not one strand of Spanish moss drooped from its limbs, nor was there a speck of lichen mottling on any part of its rough trunk. Given the warm climate and coastal fog, this was very strange. It had developed none of the parasites common to oaks of the northern California coast.

So the tree stood alone, its black-green leaves glistening as if freshly lacquered, its branches stretching out.

Galen Hendry almost had it—the melody bobbing near his threshhold of consciousness. Dum, dee, dum . . . So close, now; but the noise in the classroom increased to a din, jarring the elusive tune from his head.

Brrrrring. The din died as the bell rang.

"Thank God, it's the Governor calling," he joked lamely to Pat, the classroom aide, as he slumped down on the corner of the teacher's desk. He closed his eyes and massaged the bridge of his nose with his thumb and forefinger, trying to pull the melody back.

"W-w-w . . ."

Someone was touching Galen's knee. He opened his eyes.

Bobby peered up at him through thick glasses, a blue mustache smeared across his upper lip. "W-wake up, teacher," the chubby boy stammered, "t-t-t . . . time to go home." He patted Galen's knee affectionately with his stubby fingers. "T-time to go— "

"I know, Bobby, I know" Galen said, escorting the boy to the door of the special ed trailer. Outside Pat had the rest of the class boarding the bus.

"Bye, bye, teacher."

"Goodbye, Bobby," Galen answered, watching the boy shuffle slowly out to the curb and waiting bus. Bobby always had all the time in the world.

Galen finally turned back, his eyes sweeping over the mess—wads of butcher paper thrown about, overturned jars of poster paint, dirty brushes scattered everywhere. What a disaster. He should've saved time for cleanup instead of playing name-that-tune with himself.

"Oh, no, Galen." It was Jaime Morris, the classroom teacher. She peeked in at what was left of her room, making Galen feel like a student guilty of a class misdemeanor. She leaned against the door jamb, arms crossed over her chest, shaking her head in disbelief. "Boy, it must've been at least a nine on the Richter."

"I guess it got a way from me, Jaime," Galen said, shrugging apologetically. "I didn't watch the time. I'll stay over and help clean up." He sighed and added, "I just don't know if I'm actually going to survive the whole year— "

"Hey, Bub," the young woman said, smiling, "forget the big cleanup. Let's go over to the Blue Willow. I'm springing for tea and whatever." She brushed at the wrinkles in her white blouse and ran her fingers through her short, kinky, brown hair. "Come on." She took Galen's arm, marching him down the trailer steps, then across Taner Street to the cafe facing St. Helena Elementary School.

Inside the Blue Willow Jaime ordered a pot of herbal tea for them. "Hey, don't worry about it," she counseled, pouring the tea. "Most teachers get the first year blues—feel ineffective, even consider quitting. Special ed is even worse, the kids more demanding, more problems— "

"Ah, Jaime," Galen interrupted, "you know it's more than that. Hell, I'm not a teacher. I'm not prepared in any way. Only a provisional art credential."

"Prepared?" She chuckled. "None of us are really prepared. Do you think education courses—or even student teaching—help much?" She held up her hand and continued. "No one is prepared, Galen. Oh, it may be a little tougher for you, being itinerant, seeing all kinds of disabilities, but hang in there, bub. A year from now you'll be tough and scarred like the rest of us." She grinned, her eyes radiating confidence. "It *do* get easier."

Galen nodded, then sipped his tea.

"Now, forget the kids," Jaime ordered in a mock stern voice. "How's the art coming? Back to sketching yet?"

Galen rubbed his right hand, massaging the stiffened fingers. The drugs helped the pain, but he had not been able to do any art since the arthritis had hit his hands over a year ago. He'd given up trying. "Oh, pretty well. I haven't got back to my drawing board yet, but the exercises are helping." He dropped his hands out of sight into his lap.

Jaime nodded and changed the subject. She enthusiastically described the preparations for a backpacking trip planned for the Sierra during Easter vacation with her friend Stan, an aging mountain climber. The conversation lulled as they sipped their tea. Then Jaime mentioned something about Lynn, Galen's wife, and their property on Oakwood Lane near Napa.

Glancing at his watch, Galen groaned and jumped up from the table. He'd forgotten! "Hey, Jaime, thanks for the tea and everything. I've got to go by the old place today on the way home and put up a for-sale sign. We've got an ad in the *Register*."

He dashed across Taner and slid into the bucket seat of his yellow VW Beetle. He waived at Jaime as he pulled away from the curb. She stood on the curb in front of the Blue Willow, laughing and waving. Great gal, Galen thought, easy-going, helpful. . . .

Pushing the VW down Highway 29 from St. Helena south toward Napa, Galen tried to concentrate on the scenery. He slowed for the villages of Oakville and then Rutherford, the wine country flashing by the windows of the Volks. Occasional clusters of wood-framed farm buildings interrupted the geometry of the grapevines, rows of gnarly vine stock stretching away from the highway through a continuous carpet of blooming mustard, the rows stopping against the oak-dotted, rolling hills that framed the Napa Valley. Looks like rain, he decided, after spotting the heavy, gray clouds easing over the western hills, blowing in from the nearby Pacific. He'd have to hurry and get the sign up before it was too dark. He shifted in the seat and took a deep breath, realizing he was bone-tired. That last period had been an ordeal. Most of his classes were a breeze compared to Jaime's. Well, he wouldn't have to contend with them again until next Tuesday.

Galen shook his head, smiling wryly at his own naivete. Before last September he'd believed that retarded people often possessed unusual aptitude for art. The idea was probably an example of a belief in a kind of *law-of-compensation*, similar to the popular idea that the blind have exceptional hearing when actually they are just forced to maximize their use of normal hearing. From Galen's short experience (six months) as an itinerant art teacher with Napa County's Office of Special Education, he'd learned it was more like a *law-of-correlation*: If a kid were disabled in one area, the chances were good he was short-changed elsewhere, too. And indeed, multi-handicaps were the rule with his students. Often the secondary handicap was an emotional problem. Galen frowned. Of course his retarded students were no more artistically talented than anyone else. . . . At least *he* hadn't stimulated any young Picassos. But maybe that was his fault. He'd seen many of the good classroom teachers, like Jaime, stimulate remarkable achievements, the results often astonishing—

He hit the brakes, spotting the road sign, and turned off 29 onto Oakwood Lane, driving slowly down the bumpy county road until it ended at the driveway to an imposing two-story Victorian. It had been the original farmhouse in the area and was still known as the old Jamison Place, the maiden name of his maternal grandmother. Galen slowed for the driveway bump right next to the magnificient old live oak, slamming his brakes hard as he glimpsed something in the driveway. He flipped open the door and looked back. There, chalked across the mouth of the driveway, was a drawing. An image of Rennie, his daughter, flashed into Galen's head—a smiling round face, shiny wide brown eyes, and cheeks a brushed rose. Good God. He couldn't resist the impulse to stare up into the oak tree where she'd died just a little over a year ago. He couldn't see the tree house through the waxy green leaves, but there was the rope ladder, half its rungs intact. Galen closed his eyes, but he still saw Rennie dangling from the rope ladder, a rung remnant twisted around her neck. . . . He snapped his eyes open, looking again at the drawing. It took him several seconds to focus. Then he shivered as he eased out of the little car, buttoning his raincoat. Galen stepped closer to the drawing. Of course there had been markings there before, white-chalked, lop-sided squares, with different-sized numbers. He swallowed hard, trying to ease the growing tightness gripping his throat, and he blinked away the tears. She hadn't played hopscotch in the driveway for a long time now.

Galen rubbed the back of his wrist across his eyes, clearing his vision. He focused again on the driveway. Wrong angle; the drawing was upside-down. He moved around the short, straight chalked markings until they took recognizable shape. It was a stylized figure of a man. The figure was bent over, gazing down at something—Even from a side view the man was obviously faceless—not a dot for an eye or a slash for a mouth. Faceless. A strange lack of detail. The whole thing struck him as very primitive, crude, just the type of thing a . . .a child might do. The chill cut through his raincoat as he thought of his daughter again. He sucked in a deep breath and forced the image from his mind. Then he kneeled and touched the drawing. Chalk, expensive green chalk. He recalled Lynn's nightmares which had forced them to move. *She's still here, Galen, and she needs something from us. The tree is holding her spirit.*

Crazy.

He resisted looking back up into the tree and hurried to the VW. Who had done the drawing, and why? He could think of no answers. At the car he shrugged off the questions and the chill. It was getting dark.

Galen opened the Volks door and took the for-sale sign from the back seat. He pounded it into the ground in a soft spot under the live oak. Working under the tree added to his creepy feeling, realizing that the tree house and rope ladder hung over his head, like something ominous. Like a guillotine.

He hurried and finished with the sign. If we can't sell it in a month or so, he told himself, we'll give it to a realtor. Be best for everyone to get rid of the place. Galen straightened and looked up at the old house. The place had been elegant once, but now it needed a lot of work. The old-fashioned wooden gutters were rotted away, paint peeling everywhere.

When they'd first moved in over two years ago they hadn't had a dime to fix much of anything. He'd just graduated from the University of

Minnesota, and after moving to the Valley he'd been busy trying to make a name with his pen and inks.

A sudden movement in a second-story window caught his eye. Rennie's room. For a moment Galen thought he saw a round, pale face drawing back into the room's darkness. *She's still here.* . . . But he realized it was only a curtain fluttering in the breeze. He stood still for a moment staring and feeling embarrassed by his silliness. Then it dawned on him that the window was open and it shouldn't have been. Strange. Maybe I should check it, he thought—but he did not have a flashlight. He'd have to return tomorrow. Maybe I'll give the sheriff a call, too, he thought. There could be squatters . . . or kids partying, tearing up stuff. He climbed back into the VW, deciding to return the next afternoon and go through the house. He backed out of the driveway, over the drawing, and headed for Napa.

At the apartment complex in Napa Galen pulled into his stall, noticing that Lynn's place was empty. Probably over at the church, he guessed. For the last year his wife had spent most of her time at First Gospel attending meetings, working on church projects, distributing literature or praying for Rennie.

Galen pushed open the apartment door and stopped in his tracks.

Lynn was sitting in the dark, her coat buttoned up to her neck, two suitcases at her feet. Her face was pale and drawn, the permanently wounded look glazing her brown eyes.

He whispered, "Lynn? Are you okay Lynn?"

She nodded. With an effort she stood. "Aunt Jane's driving the Volvo. She took some of my things to her place," Lynn explained, her monotone matching her appearance. "She'll be back soon . . ." Her voice trailed off and she looked down at her suitcases.

"What's going on?" asked Galen.

Lynn looked up but avoided his eyes, looking out the front window of the apartment. "I'm leaving, Galen," she said simply, "going to Mother's in the city."

He waited for her to continue.

After an awkward silence, Lynn whispered, "We don't really share much anymore, Galen. Aunt Jane says—"

Goddammit. Galen swore silently, shutting out his wife's voice. He was sick of hearing what Aunt Jane had to say about everything. The old lady had involved Lynn with the church and encouraged the craziness about Rennie. She'd even convinced Lynn that the little girl's accident related to a series of bizarre deaths at the old Victorian, the earliest recorded in the 1800's when the Jamisons hung a half-breed from the live oak for stock rustling: he'd been innocent. Lynn's nightmares about Rennie included the image of a man's face, horribly bloated and discolored. Anyhow, she said it was the tree. A haunted tree? No, he'd had enough of the old lady's meddling. Lynn was dabbing at her nose with a hankie. ". . . and Andrew will be contacting you in a few days," she murmured, shifting her gaze back to the suitcases, "you know, about legal and financial details . . ."

Andrew, her cousin—Handelman, Brooks and Brooks of San Francisco. Galen stared at his wife. She had been a beautiful woman, charming and lively, before all this. She blamed herself for Rennie's death because she'd been gone that day on her new job. Galen had never been able to tell her the whole truth. Now it was too late. The words were buried inside him.

Honk, honk.

That's her now, Galen thought, feeling deflated.

"Goodbye, Galen," Lynn said, picking up her suitcases, then slipping quickly past him and out the door.

"Goodbye," he whispered softly, as the door shut.

After a moment, Galen took off the raincoat and hung it on the door of the closet. Then, unloosening his tie, he wandered into the kitchen and made a cup of instant coffee. He added a generous slug of brandy. As an afterthought he rummaged through the back of the junk drawer, finding his good stuff, Humbolt Indica, hidden in a Skoal can. He rolled a joint, lit up, and inhaled deeply, holding the smoke in his lungs until tiny, invisible fingers began massaging away the tightness and fatigue from his body; then he exhaled. With the joint dangling from his mouth and the cup of coffee in hand, Galen moved back to the front room. He built a roaring fire, sipping the coffee, taking hits on the joint, and waiting for some response to Lynn's departure. A sense of loss or anguish or regret—even self-pity. Nothing. His guilt of the last year had sapped his emotions, his ability to respond strongly to anything. Well, that's not quite true, he told himself, because he did feel something—relief. He was actually glad Lynn was gone. He tossed the butt into the flames. The fire cracked.

Galen slumped down in his recliner, sipping coffee. He flipped on the TV with the remote control, watching a face focus on the screen. He finished the last of the coffee, trying to concentrate on the sportscaster. But he couldn't. Something nagged at him.

Rennie's mural.

Galen had finally gotten a break, signed a good contract for six pen and ink drawings of Napa Valley landmarks with a specialty card company in San Francisco that planned to reproduce them on post cards. To celebrate they'd decided to use some of the up-front money to fix up Rennie's room—patch the original plaster, replace moldings and put on a fresh coat of paint. They started on Friday night after Lynn got off from her new job at Queen of the Valley Hospital. By Sunday morning they were ready for the first coat of latex. At noon Galen left the roller in the five gallon paint bucket and went downstairs to devour a tuna sandwich and glass of milk. He was putting the dishes in the sink when he heard Lynn shout: "Oh, no, Rennie!"

Then silence.

Galen dashed back up the staircase and down the hall to his daughter's room, not knowing what to expect. Lynn was sitting in the middle of the floor, tears running down her cheeks. She gestured at Rennie. The little three-year-old girl had a felt marking pen in hand. And the walls—the walls were decorated with a mural of green stick figures. Galen sunk to the floor as if hit over the head. "Good God," he moaned, putting his arm around Lynn's shoulders.

Rennie smiled proudly at her parents. "Da-dee, Rennie draws too." She pointed to the stick figures with the green marking pen.

Struck dumb, Galen just nodded. Then they began to laugh together. They'd left the stick-figure mural on the walls.

The following Monday Galen had barely noticed Lynn leaving for work. He'd heard her say, "Keep an eye on Rennie; you know how she gets into stuff." But his attention was on the set of drawings for the card company. After his wife left he ignored the sound of the front door opening and closing. Rennie would be okay outside for a few minutes. . . . Finally he put the finishing touches on the last pen and ink. When he glanced at his watch, Lynn had been gone two hours. And Rennie— she'd been unattended all that time.

Galen had rushed out the door, shouting her name.

At the oak he'd stopped suddenly, as if he'd run into an invisible wall. It was unreal. Rennie looked like a rag doll, her head bent at a funny angle, dangling from the rope ladder, twisting in the breeze. Unreal. . . .

He'd climbed the rope ladder, cut her down and called the paramedics, but it was too late. A freak accident, they said. Apparently she'd been climbing the ladder when a rung gave way, the loose end becoming tangled around her neck. He'd never told anyone about the two hours— he couldn't. After the funeral Lynn began having the terrible nightmares. He vowed to cut the tree down, but then the arthritis hit.

In the kitchen Galen poured himself another straight shot of brandy. He massaged the aching knuckles of his right hand. After awhile he went to bed; but he tossed and turned, his rest disturbed by the image of a rag doll twisting in the breeze.

The next morning Galen walked into the staff lounge of the County Office, saying hello to one of the adaptive physical education teachers. He poured himself a cup of coffee and sat down to check his schedule for the day, making sure there were no field trips or other changes. None. Morning classes at Wintun, the TMR school in Napa, and the afternoon at Theodore Roosevelt, the PH school in Yountville. He made a mental note to stop by and check out the house on Oakwood on the way home. Damn, he'd forgotten to call the sheriff last night. Probably no need, really.

Galen's thoughts were disturbed by a discussion between a speech therapist and an ESL teacher. A kid with a problem. ". . . it must be a kind of expressive aphasia," the speech therapist was saying. "All the tests check."

Maria Espinoza, the ESL teacher, nodded, her concern easing. "Dr. Raintree will be at my class at State tonight," she said, enthusiasm edging into her tone. "Maybe he can help design a remedial program for Peter."

The speech therapist smiled and nodded. Galen had heard similar discussions in the lounge or teachers' rooms of various schools in the county. After a kid's problem was labeled there was usually a sense of relief, because it was believed that somewhere, perhaps just down the hall, there was an *expert* who could cure *that* problem. Unfortunately the labels were vague, poorly defined: aphasia, autism, dyslexia, low-achiever, developmentally-delayed, educationally-handicapped. Galen had learned to ignore most of this, focusing instead on Jaime Morris's practical advice: Forget their disabilitites and focus on what they *can* do. She had dramatically demonstrated the principle by taking Galen to a sheltered workshop for adult TMRs. The shop was run by a retired Navy chief with no training in educational philosophy or psychology and no interest in labeling. The workshop had a contract assembling first-aid kits for Johnson. The problem was that none of the workers could read or count accurately. The Chief had designed a board with silhouettes of each kit item: five bandaids, a large compress, a package of ammonia capsules, a bottle of aspirins, and so on. Each worker covered the silhouettes on his board first, then filled each kit from the covered board. Focus on what they can do.

"Morning, Galen."

He glanced up from his coffee cup into Anne Jurgensen's face. "Hi, Anne." He pointed at an empty seat next to him.

She shook her head, indicating the letter in hand, frowning. "Did you get yours?"

He shrugged his lack of understanding.

"A March Fifteenth letter?"

"Oh . . . I didn't check my box." He'd forgotten that many teachers across the State were receiving the demoralizing letters today. In the hall he leaned over and checked his box. He had a letter. He tore it open:

Mr. Galen Hendry
21 Oakwood Lane
Napa, CA 94558

Dear Mr. Hendry,

Pursuant to the California State Education Code, you are advised that at this time economic conditions do not warrant renewing your contract for the next school year (July 1980 – June 1981). The sole intent of this letter is to provide an opportunity for you to seek a position elsewhere for the next school year.

Regretfully,
John D. Martin
Superintendent
Napa County Schools

Attached to the outside of the envelope was a note scrawled in pen: *Galen, see me before classes today. JDM*

"Hey, it's just a formality, Galen." Anne had followed him to his box and patted his shoulder. "Half the teachers in the county have received them for the last three years. It's a negotiating ploy before each new contract. And anyhow, all first-year teachers get them."

Actually Galen didn't feel much of anything—except curiosity about the note from Martin. "Everyone get one of these?" He let Anne read the note.

She shook her head, perplexed. "Well, good luck, Galen. Let me know how it comes out."

He nodded, turned, and headed down the hall to the main reception area. Mrs. Wallace the receptionist ushered him right into the superintendent's office.

Martin, behind a big desk, set his pipe down as Galen entered the room. "Have a seat," the superintendent said with a fake smile. Behind him the American and California flags hung limply from modified stanchions.

Galen slumped into the chair in front of the big desk.

"Well," Martin began, digging through a stack of papers on his desk, "there's really no kind way to do this." He cleared his throat, holding up a letter and shaking it, as if it were a naughty puppy. "The endowment which enabled us to hire an art specialist for special education has run out and will not be renewed by the State." He let the unruly letter drop to his desk top. "Your position won't exist next year." He shook his head and added, not unkindly, "Your March Fifteenth letter must be taken seriously."

"I see." Galen did not know what else to say.

After several seconds of silence, Martin continued. "Of course I'll be happy to give you a strong recommendation if you find something elsewhere. Unfortunately, I anticipate no other teaching opportunities with the County next year." He paused and packed his pipe carefully. After lighting it, he stood and offered Galen his hand. That was that.

Leaving the County office, Galen thought: I'm unemployed. Out of work in a couple of months. He rubbed his right hand, which ached. What the hell was he going to do after June? An artist who couldn't use his hands with a degree in art history; his options seemed limited at best. Maybe something at the junior college? No. He had to admit he'd been an ineffective teacher even with students who were *not* prone to criticism. And college students. . . .

That afternoon, after his last class at Theodore Roosevelt, Galen drove straight to the old Jamison place. He parked the VW under the oak and slid out of the bucket seat, glancing up at the house. Damn. Rennie's window was closed! Now that was strange. He was sure it'd been open last night. He shook his head and moved around the car, stopping short of the chalked drawing. He'd expected the man with no face to be gone, washed away by last night's rain. But it was still there . . . and more. The figure was kneeling, staring down, but more elaborate, the angular lines softened, brushed slightly, making the drawing less crude, more subtle. Still, the man lacked a face; and now, in a more sophisticated sketch, the lack of detail was even more striking. Galen studied the changes technically: the artist had added more lines, cleverly varying length, using different degrees of pressure on the chalk and brushing for tone, but he found no use of curves. Curious. . . . And there was some background added behind the figure: a tree, its lines soft, undefined.

Galen turned slightly to his left and stepped back into the street, looking up at the live oak, comparing it to the drawing. Of course it matched. Who was doing this? he asked himself.

Still puzzled, Galen returned to the Volks and picked up the watchman's flashlight. Then he walked up the driveway. Kids? No, that didn't really square with the growing technical competence of the chalked drawing. . . . No, it wasn't a kid's prank. He walked up the steps of the old house, caution slowing his stride. He paused and listened intently at the front door. Nothing. I wish I had called the sheriff, Galen thought, feeling even more uneasy as the front door creaked open.

Late afternoon, gloomy silence and musty smelling.

In the front room Galen checked all the windows. Locked. Everything appeared secure. He went through each room on the ground floor, finding nothing disturbed, the furniture draped with sheets just as they'd left it. The kitchen, pantry and sewing room were in perfect order. Galen paused in his studio, the emptiness closing in on him, increasing his unease. The last time he'd worked in this room was *that* day. He put the flashlight under his arm and blew on his cold fingers. Then he took a deep breath, closing his eyes. *Rennie, her brown eyes glistening.* Oh, God. He snapped open his eyes. I'm going around the bend, just like Lynn. He hurried out of the room.

Climbing the staircase to the second floor, Galen ran his hand along the smoothly-worn hand rail, his shifting weight making each riser creak noisily. He shook his head as if warding off a pesky mosquito. The sun must've dipped behind the hills, he thought, noticing that the afternoon gloom had darkened the second floor. He flipped on the big flashlight and checked the guest bedroom—windows locked, everything secure. Then he followed the yellow beam into the master bedroom—nothing disturbed. Down the hall to the other guest bedroom—okay, not even a wrinkle on the sheet over the bed. Finally he moved to the end of the hall, the last door—Rennie's room. He paused, his heart thumping against his ribs. He hadn't been inside the room since her funeral. After taking several deep breaths, the tightness eased slightly in his chest. He pushed open the door slowly, swinging the light around the room: Rennie's toy chest, her rocking horse, the clown paintings he'd done special for her. He moved closer to the mural on the walls; the stick figures were similar to the first man-with-no-face drawings. He shook his head. *That* thought was crazy—

A noise startled him.

Galen flashed the light on Rennie's bed. The covering was bunched, wrinkled, half on the floor—and something had moved under the bed. He swallowed hard, jumping back as something darted across the floor for the open door. A ball of orange fur—Rennie's pet cat.

"Rhubarb, Rhubarb," he shouted, following the animal out the door. But it was too late; the frightened cat was gone, down the staircase. . . . The pet had disappeared shortly after Rennie's funeral and they'd assumed it was dead. Obviously not. Had it been around here for a year? Galen shivered; he was cold and tired.

Downstairs he slumped onto the couch, not even bothering to remove the white sheets. The cat reminded him of happier times. Lynn had brought Rhubarb home when they were still in Minnesota. . . .

It had been the time of the annual St. Paul Winter Carnival. Lynn had bundled the two-year-old Rennie in a bulky snowsuit and taken her to a nearby park to see the elaborate ice sculptures. She chased the little toddler across the drawbridge of an ice castle, along the ramparts, down a tower, through a courtyard and back across the solid moat. The roly-poly two-year-old scrambled up the side of a huge bear and scooted down its backside, a tiny kitten joining her. Lynn finally caught up near Snow White and the Dwarves. The two rested on their backs, cheeks a strawberry red, gasping geysers of mist into the air as the kitten climbed over them. A TV cameraman had recorded it all and Galen and Lynn had watched it as an overlay on the 11:00 o'clock news. They'd made love on the couch in front of the TV, giggling at each other's goose-pimpled nakedness and the little orange kitten that wanted to join the play.

Galen forced himself up off the couch. Outside the house, he stopped near the chalk drawing. How could Rennie do this? It was ridiculous, but he was convinced that somehow the drawing related to his dead daughter. He climbed back into the Volks.

The sky was dark and overcast at the end of Oakwood Lane. From his spot under the live oak, Galen could barely see the house. He pulled the blanket tighter around his shoulders, then leaned forward and poured himself another cup of brandy-laced coffee. Sipping the hot drink, he settled down in the canvas chair, leaning back against the trunk of the tree. He blinked back tears. What am I doing here? he asked himself. Earlier it had seemed like such a good idea to sneak out here and set up a stakeout. He'd parked the VW on 29 just at dark and hiked in, carrying the chair, blanket, thermos and a couple of joints, careful to keep out of sight of the old Jamison place. But after two hours of sitting in the cold and getting loaded, the idea seemed pretty stupid. He wasn't sure now what he'd expected to find out. Too much TV. He leaned away from the trunk and checked the mouth of the driveway—he couldn't actually see the drawings from here, but he'd spot anyone coming up. So far, nothing.

The buzz from the dope was wearing off and the brandy was making him sleepy. . . .

Galen's eyes blinked open. Confused, his reactions slowed, he struggled up out of the canvas chair. Someone was at the drawing, someone very small. He blinked. The figure dissolved to a ball . . . the ball moved toward him.

"Ahhh," he shouted, lifting his arms to shield his face. But the ball of fur dashed by Galen and up the tree. He blinked again, rubbing his eyes. Had he been dreaming? Maybe it was Rhubarb, he wasn't sure. He was unsteady on his feet, sweaty under the heavy blanket. He let the cover slip from his shoulders and moved closer to check the drawing.

The figure's position had been changed, more frontal now, the face exposed to view. Head cocked, the figure appeared to be listening to something. On the ground was a piece of chalk. Galen picked it up. His fingers felt supple, alive. He kneeled and made a few tentative strokes. Gaining confidence, he began to sketch boldly. First the facial details, eyebrows, eyes, nose, mouth. Then the more subtle marks of expression:

a lined forehead, crow's feet at the corners of the eyes, the deep creases around the mouth. Sketch, smudge, soften. He worked furiously for several minutes, the chalk detailing the features from his subconscious mind's eye. The creative outburst was finally complete. Galen sucked in his breath: It was his own face! He had regained his touch, the arthritis gone. The nature of the drawing was clear. The figure was looking down at a drawing, but something—a sound from behind?—had caused the figure to look up and turn slightly.

Suddenly he had the creepy feeling of being watched.

Then he heard something from up in the tree. He turned slightly, cocking his head, listening. At that moment he realized he was striking the pose from the drawing at his feet. Something very strange was taking place—

A voice from the treehouse, hardly more than a whisper, "Da-dee, Da-dee. . . ."

Good God, it was her. "I'm coming, Baby, I'm coming," he shouted, struggling up the old rope ladder. Up, up he pulled himself, tears blurring his vision. Then he saw it. A face. He brushed aside a limb. It was Rennie—

No: her features dissolved, replaced by a man. A man grinning, his face puffy and discolored a dark indigo . . . and fading. Nothing there but rough tree trunk.

Snap. A rung gave way and Galen was falling . . . falling, something tangling around his neck, growing tighter, tighter. And as the blackness closed in, he knew Aunt Jane had been right.

THE GOLD COIN

by

MORRIS WEISS

In New York City in the early nineteen hundreds you could buy a large schooner of beer for a nickle. A free lunch came with it. This morning Jake the tailor was first at the teller's window. He laid down a five-dollar bill.

"Mister please give me a gold piece, a shiny one if you got it. It's my grandson's bar mitzvah present."

Jake was a young-looking grandfather. Tall and slim, his brown hair and pin-striped mustache were just starting to turn grey. His blue eyes examined the shiny gold piece. It was about the size of a penny.

Hurrying out of the bank, his long strides soon brought him to his cleaning store. It was a small place: a sewing machine beside the entrance, a pressing board with hand iron in the center. The customers' clothes hung on racks in the rear.

Jake rolled up the sleeves on his white shirt and put the clothes brush on his striped trousers. Jake always dressed like the matinee idol he once dreamt he would be. Now he began his ten-hour work day. Two o'clock: his wife, Ida, brought hot soup and sandwiches. She was a short, wiry brunette with good features, except for her nose, which was a bit too long. They sat at the sewing machine and used it as a table.

"Two more weeks," smiled Jake, "our Louis will have his bar mitzvah."

"Thirteen years already," sighed Ida. "He's supposed to be a man. Yes, maybe in the old country. Here the children come to the parents till they are middle-aged."

While Jake and Ida were chatting this Thursday afternoon, a badly

100

crippled beggar was making his rounds. A tombstone must have fallen on the poor man. He had a brace on his twisted knee. On his right foot he wore a large-heeled orthopedic shoe. The right side of his face was flattened in. His right ear was a mass of discolored skin. There are many handicapped people limping along. However, what was unusual about this beggar was his right arm. It was only half an arm. His fingers dangled limply where his elbow should have been.

After canvassing the city for many years, the old beggar established a route. Each day he covered specific territory, making stops like a rent collector. Every Thursday about three o'clock he was at Jake's door. He had been doing it for years. When Jake would see him he would hurry over and give him a penny.

This Thursday after lunch Ida went home. Three o'clock the beggar opened Jake's door as usual. Jake was at the door talking to a customer. He quickly handed the beggar a coin.

Later that evening Jake was fumbling for the gold piece. He took out all his change, but it was not there.

"Givalt, my heavens," he screamed, "I lost it."

Ida scrambled out of bed.

"Jake, what happened? What happened Jake?"

"Louis's gold piece. The gold piece is gone. "

"Stay calm Jake. You never lose anything. Look again."

Jake held out all his change.

"Look, it's not here. That's it."

"Yolt, stupid," shouted Ida, "Who puts a gold piece together mit pennies and nickles? You must've given it to someone."

"Wait, wait," exclaimed Jake, "I gave it to the old beggar. Maybe he won't notice it."

"Dumbell," shouted Ida. "Who won't notice a gold piece from a penny?"

"Maybe he'll bring it back next Thursday," said Jake.

Ida grimaced. "Bring it back? He should live so long."

The loss kept Jake awake half the night. In those days some people worked all week for five dollars. It was a long wait till Thursday came again. That day Ida stayed after lunch. Three o'clock, four, five: the beggar did not show.

"Five years," grumbled Jake. "Never missed a Thursday. Now I'm positive he got it."

"I was already positive last week." said Ida.

Jake gritted his teeth. "Even if it costs me money, I'll find that son-of-a bitch."

The neighborhood learned of Jake's calamity and of his determination to locate the beggar. A couple of people had seen the beggar at one time or another. Monday morning Joe, a cab-driver, came into the store.

"I work the night shift," he told Jake, "six o'clock I take the subway to get my cab. A couple of times that beggar was on the train. He got off at Pitkin Ave., so he must live around there."

"Joe, please try to find out where he lives."

That night when Joe was near the Pitkin Ave. station he pulled into the taxi stand. He asked the other taxi drivers. One responded.

"That crippled man lives in that big house three blocks up the street."

Joe drove there. It was a big corner apartment building with two entrances. He stopped at the superintendent's apartment.

"Do you know the crippled man with the short arm?" he asked the super.

"He's upstairs," said the super, "perhaps I can help you."

"Thanks," said Joe, "I came to see the beggar."

The super glared at him. "Beggar," he exclaimed, "That's Mister Lilly, the landlord."

Joe hurried up to his apartment. He rang the doorbell. The beggar opened the door as far as the inner latch allowed.

"The tailor wants his gold piece," said Joe. "He will be here to see you."

The beggar pulled out his wallet and peeled out four single dollar bills. He took out a handful of change and counted out ninety-nine cents.

BY THE NUMBERS

by

FRANK CRISCENTI

So many names—some people I've never seen: "Do you know a Martinez at 1099?" Barney, my boss, asks.

"Sure," I say, and he hands me a misaddressed letter. But I've never seen Martinez. I know his mail, I know the thin letters he receives from Mexico, but I don't know Martinez.

Mexicans, Central Americans, Vietnamese, a few black people, a few white people, and the old residences. Dusty front yards. Half the yards are dusty in this neighborhood. In the other yards, behind cinder-block walls, behind ornate ironwork gates, roses peak out between the black metal. Geraniums prosper. Vegetable gardens produce golden squash flowers and yellow tomato blossoms.

The smells of cooking pots full of meats, tomatoes and chilis waft from the kitchens.

Dark-eyed, black-haired children, old enough to be in school, follow me. I ignore them or they'll follow me the whole block, asking questions, giving information:

"They're not home."

And: "Do you have any letters for my cousin?"

Sloe-eyed, shy Latin señoritas wait, but not for me.

Torres's market stands on the corner, near El Camino, selling two-for-a-nickel candy, fresh tortillas, soda pops. I'll drink two or three sodas during the worst heat. The kids stand out in front, pointing and giggling at my skinny legs below my shorts. The kids are always coming, always going, always choosing in deadly earnest from among the two-for-a-nickel candies, considering the various colors like stock options. Old women dressed for another time, another world, picking out the fresh tortillas by the dozen. This world is more theirs than mine.

The young dudes drive bright, shiny cars; but the cars, no matter how bright, how shiny, rarely go fast enough to escape the neighborhood. So the young dudes stay, and on Saturday afternoons they watch me, drinking Bud and booting a soccer ball back and forth in the dust. They gossip loudly over the train whistles.

I'm almost done for the day, and I'm early as well. My mail pouch grows lighter as I stop at each house, at the beat-up apartments, at the dilapidated duplexes, as I pass the old men sitting on rickety front porches wearing hats with brightly colored woven hat bands. I'm sweating, though it's only just warm.

Pass the two condemned houses, then half of this sleepy block, and I'm done. As I approach the property, with its rotting fence and overgrown yard, I see her. I've never seen her before. She's wearing a large, Japanese-style, floppy straw hat tied with a scarf, and digging in the dust with a hoe.

WARNING

NO TRESPASSING

This property has been

CONDEMNED

by the County of San Mateo.

The front door is wide open and the sign is there, right next to the door, the NO TRESPASSING and CONDEMNED painted in bright red. I stare at the woman, but she doesn't seem to notice. She raises the hoe a little ways and lets it fall to the earth, cutting a brown smile into the hard, tan ground. She raises it again, and it falls. Her skin is well-tanned, her legs looking like knotted ropes beneath her print dress. The handle of the hoe is smooth from sweat and friction.

I've got to report her to someone; she's living in a condemned house, after all. I'm still staring at her, but she won't notice me. I'll finish the rest of the block and tell the boss about her when I return to the office. Let Barney handle it; that's the proper thing to do. She's trying to get away with something. Someone's always trying to get away with something.

But when I finish I decide to go back. She just can't stay there. She's so ancient looking, not frail, but old, this knotted woman working under the shade of the straw hat. Someone should tell her. I walk back and stand at the crumbling fence, but she won't notice me, won't look up. I try to get her to notice my official, government-issue evil eye. I know she knows I'm there.

"Do you realize that this house is condemned?" I ask, figuring such a question to be a good place to start.

She doesn't answer but looks up, staring at me with ink-blue eyes, riveting me to the spot, disorienting me, her face firm against its own wrinkles. She has a noble nose that she itches with a gloved finger. An old white woman in a condemned house in this neighborhood? What's she doing here?

The hoe rises and falls.

"Do you speak English? You can't stay here, it's condemned," I try, but I feel kind of stupid now. I'll just inform the authorities. It's the proper thing to do.

"I live here." Her accent is thick but the words are spoken with conviction. The hoe rises and falls.

"But you can't. This place is condemned, don't you understand?"

She looks up again briefly with those eyes, perturbed. The hoe bites deeper into the dust and the hard ground underneath. "I live here," she says, without looking up.

I play my trump card. "Can't you read?" It's a deliberate insult maybe, but I'm a Government Employee and occasionally entitled to the rudeness the public attributes to us. "The sign says no trespassing."

The hoe rises and falls.

"Really. This place is condemned. You've got to leave."

She works the hoe quickly a few more times and then smooths out the clumps of hard dirt. Then she turns and walks slowly into the house.

I follow her and I don't know why. I question myself as I do, trespassing like this onto condemned land. I walk up the cracked concrete pathway, careful to stay off the garden she's worked. I knock on the cracked door jamb, the residue of faded grey paint sticking to my knuckles.

"I am here."

I go into the house. A thin white dust from the deteriorating drywall covers what's left of the walls and floors. The hallway is cool, and I can see much of the house from there. In some places there are no floors; you can see the ground through the rotting slats. The doors to the rooms are either missing or hung lop-sided, half off their hinges. The house is full of debris: old newspapers, damp cardboard boxes and broken wallboard. Filthy, striped wallpaper hangs in one of the rooms. Maybe something has crawled under this place and died; it smells of decay, mold, rodents and urine. The aroma of hot tea competes with the stench.

I follow it into the kitchen. The woman busies herself over a campstove on a newspaper-covered counter. The room is as clean as it can be here. There's a table covered with more newspaper, a lawn chair next to it.

"Do you want tea?" she asks.

I nod and mutter something sounding like Yes.

She brings an ancient flowered china tea-pot and two teacups to the table. Taking the teacup with a chip in it for herself, she pours the tea, first into my cup, then hers. I'm trying not to look at her. In the corner there's a broken three-legged chair which looks like it might bear my weight. Bringing it to the table I test it gently before covering it with a sheet of clean newspaper and sitting. She brings some matzo crackers to the table on a chipped plate.

"Thank you." I really don't know what to say now.

She sits silently, not looking at me but staring off at the walls. When she raises her teacup I notice the numbers tattooed above her wrist.

One day when I worked as a messenger in San Francisco, I found myself packed close in an elevator with all these people in suits and ties. I was in a T-shirt and Levi's, feeling dirty. It was an old elevator, the kind needing an operator. I looked at him as he worked the levers and saw the same numbers on his arm. They were visible underneath the sleeve of his uniform when he pushed the lever. I thought of him standing there all day. Those numbers would show and not show, visible and invisible, as he pushed and pulled the lever. I couldn't look at his face, just the numbers.

She notices me doing the same thing, staring at her arm, and looks up at me. We exchange a glance, and with it a certain elemental level of understanding. I *know* where she got it, but I will never know the pain it represents. Her look tells me that, and more.

I sip my tea and absent-mindedly take a bite of the flavorless cracker. I'm stumped.

"You know you can't stay here. When they find you they'll kick you out."

She looks off into the distance again, her face set, grim and stubborn. She doesn't get up to leave, just sits and sips her tea, teeth grinding on the matzo.

"Don't you have any family?" I ask.

She looks up and stares through me at the door, as if expecting someone to come in. It seemed to me that, after all these years, there must be *someone*.

It's Monday, and I've been away for a three-day weekend. I'm nearing the condemned houses on my route. The old lady has been there for about three weeks now. She's made the earth browner, richer. Green shoots had just begun to peek out from the ground before I had started my days off, and I'm anxious to see the progress of her garden.

I pull out thin letters from Guatemala for this house, thin letters from Mexico for the next, and then I see it. I shove letters into boxes as quickly as I can, not wanting to waste any steps. Perhaps my eyes have failed me in this blasted heat. They're not there. The condemned houses are not there.

Huge tire ruts have scarred the earth. Shards of broken glass and remnants of snapped two-by-fours litter the ground. Still, green shoots struggle through the debris. Nestled among them is a small teacup.

ICE

by

F<small>RANK</small> W<small>ARE</small>

It was winter of '68. Down the highway from Las Vegas you could see a light coming closer, a light that became two lights, and which finally could be distinguished as a green V-dub squareback. The car slowed down as it neared the diner, but not slow enough for the gravel it hit. The car drifted a few feet, but it was nothing the driver couldn't handle. No one noticed it in the diner. No one except for the sheriff and his deputy.

"Did you see that sucker come in here?"

"Huh, what? Oh shit, somebody did kick up some dust, didn't they."

"It was that Volkswagen over there."

"Oh well shit. None of them Volkswagens can drive anyway."

The car pulled up. The sheriff eyed it. He saw the driver and a nerve hit. His body twitched. His eyes reached out over his coffee and out into the car. It grabbed the driver for an uncomfortable second. The driver broke it off by avoiding the stare, but he could still feel it. It affected the way he moved.

"Well look what we got here."

"Jesus, look at how long that hippie's hair is."

"I don't understand how they can wear their hair that long. I gotta cut mine, y'know? It don't feel good."

The shotgun got out of the V-dub and tucked his shirt in. His name was Rick, and the first thing that came to his mind, he said: "What do ya think the locals do around here Johnny boy?"

"I don't know, probably string up long hairs and hitchhikers."

"Yeah, more 'n likely."

"Let's get the fuck in there or I'm gonna fall asleep here. Man I could shoot that caffeine into my eyeballs."

"How can you feel like sleeping in this freeze-ass weather? I thought deserts were warm, like Palm Springs and all that."

They walked inside, and though the heater was on it was still cold. The waitress was an iceberg and the sheriff's booth was Antarctica. As soon as they came in the waitress turned her back on them and threw her eyes up back into her forehead in disgust before disappearing into the kitchen. This registered in the sheriff's head and he laughed annoyingly. Snowballs were bouncing off his grin. Rick didn't know what he was laughing about. He looked over and smiled. He nodded a hello. The sheriff's laugh broke in midstride. His face turned down in volume. His eyes became large with hate. Rick made a note of this and wrote it off.

"Where the fuck is everybody?" Rick said under his breath to John.

"The waitress must be in the back fucking the cook."

"Must be . . . ah, there she is."

"All right. I'm starved."

The cops got up and took long measured steps. With every step a weight was added to their hearts. They took an uncomfortable amount of time walking past and out the door.

"What's their trip?"

"Fucking our trip."

"Yeah, really."

The cop car burst out the parking lot and screamed out onto the highway.

"Red hot go ahead."

"Yeah, really."

*   *   *

A few minutes in the future and a few miles up the road hidden behind an overpass, tucked away out of sight, was a cream-colored, hate-filled Polora. The VW caught up with the future too soon for its own good. John was trying to pick up something halfway decent on the AM band.

"All they got around here is shitkickin' oakie crap . . . oh shit."

"What? . . . What do you see?"

"Those fuckin' pigs back at the diner. They just pulled in behind us."

"Ah shit. Where the fuckin' hell did you hide the lid?"

"In the backpack."

"Ah, real smart you dumb ass. They'll never think of looking in there, you dumb shit."

"How in the hell was I supposed to know we were gonna run into those pigs?"

"Well just fucking drive normal."

"Too late—he's got us."

"Ah shit. What for? We weren't speeding."

"Don't look back you cunt. Act normal."

"I am acting normal. Pull over."

"Jeez, that motherfucker is blinding me with them goddam lights."

"Just show him your I.D. and agree with him."

"Yeah yeah, I know."

One cop stayed at the car and aimed the light while the other one walked with a careful strangeness. John fumbled with his wallet and looked up and stared down the barrel of a gun."

"Out of the car real slow, creep."

"There must be some mistake officer."

"Shut your mouth."

The other cop ran up and commanded Rick out. They were thrown on the hood. Snap. Snap. John's ankles were kicked out from underneath him. His faced slammed onto the hood. He could see the gun out of the corner of his eye. He could feel a hand going over his body. His wrists felt a pain when they were locked together. His questions went unanswered. One of the pigs searched the car and it was over. John felt numb.

*   *   *

"Yeah hello, Barb? Yeah, all right, am I glad you're home. Now listen . . . listen. . . . No, I'm not home. Listen, I got busted . . . Barb, Barb, listen to me: I'm sure it won't stick. They blew the procedure, but you gotta get me and Rick outahere. . . . Where? Oh yeah, Barstow. . . . We're in Barstow. That's on the way to Vegas. What do you mean you don't know where it is? Find out. . . . For dope. We got busted for dope. . . . About half a lid. . . . Listen . . . will you listen? Goddam now listen. Get your ass over here and bail us out. Go over and get Steve to come with you. He'll know what to do. Get here as quick as you can. I don't want to rot in this rathole. . . . Don't worry about me, just get here . . . Bye, don't worry. . . ."

"Well, she's coming."

"Good."

*   *   *

"Hey, how come we don't get the same cell?"

"Because we don't want you two making trouble."

"How much trouble can you make in a cell?"

"Just shut up and get in."

Rick was put in a cell by himself while John was locked three doors down with four odd-looking winos.

"Hey, I don't wanna be stuck in here."

"That's too bad. Shut up and get in."

The pig locked the door and walked down the hall. He closed another door behind him and locked it. God this place smells rank, John thought. He could feel someone get too close.

"Well, what have we got here?"

John turned around and saw that he was in for something. "You got nothing. Get your fucking hand off me."

"Oh, don't Suzie look cute when she gets mad."

"HEY GUARD. GET ME THE FUCK OUTAHERE. HEY GUARD, GET ME. . . ."

Rick yelled, "Whatza matter?" He could hear a fight. The noise climaxed with a dull thud. No answer. "JOHN!"

Someone's foot kicked John's head and time spilled out of John's eyes. His senses were broken in half. He could feel the blood rush up his neck and out his mouth.

"JOHN!"

He could feel his head spin forward but he couldn't see anything but an occassional white flash that came every time he got hit.

Rick was trying to squeeze through the bars. His eyes were trying to reach around the wall. "GUARD, God help us. GUARD!" The loudness cracked his throat. Sweat broke out all over him. "GUARRD." He started to cry. He could hear his buddy getting killed and he couldn't do a thing. "GUARRD." He could see the pig down at the end of the hall behind the door. Just the back of his pig neck was all he could see through the little window. Just enough to torture him. "GUARRD." Then he saw something that hit him like a car. Blood came from John's cell and rolled toward the drain. His eyes stopped blinking. His brain stopped working. His lungs were paralyzed. The word "guard" caught in his throat. He fell on his knees and the pain began.

*   *   *

It was around 8:20 the next morning when they unlocked the door. The cop nudged Rick, who was in a daze. "Don't touch me, pig."

"You're outa jail. Two people are waiting for you."

"Yeah? Where's my buddy?"

"Oh, is he the guy that got beat up?"

"Yeah, you cocksucker."

"Now calm down. He's in the county hospital. He'll be all right."

"Yeah, well where the fuck were you guys?" The cop didn't look into Rick's eyes. "What about those assholes that attacked him?"

"Now don't you worry about them. We'll take care of them."

"Why the fuck didn't you take care of 'em last night?"

The cop didn't answer. He opened the final door. Rick could see Barb crying. The pain and shame hit him again. He looked at Steve and saw revenge flex in his jaws. They looked almost as bad as himself, having driven all night and then finding out what had happened. He took his shoes, wallet and belt. "Thanks for nothin." He turned and walked through the opening in the cage. He put his arm around Barb and she leaned on him. No one said a thing.

When they made it to the door and out into the sunlight, Rick asked: "What happened?"

Steve answered, "You tell me. His pelvis was cracked, his leg was broken, he's got a couple of broken ribs and a bunch of cuts. They buttfucked him. His asshole ain't in such great shape either."

"Shut up, goddam you." Barb covered her face. Rick tried to comfort her but she pulled away from him. Steve stepped in front of him. He stared at him. Rick didn't look back. He scratched himself nervously. "You gotta smoke?"

"Yeah." He fumbled for them. "Did you see 'em?"

"No. I was in the other cell, but I did get two of their names—Lopez and Zimmerman. I couldn't hear the rest of 'em."

"Well, no problem. We'll find them. We'll probably find out if they have a trial."

"They better fucking have one."

"Well, it won't matter. I'm gonna get Coronado, Gordy and the gang and we're gonna fucking kill 'em."

Biographies

F.N. Wright, age 47, has worked for the Postal Service for four years. He has two published novels to his credit: *Flight to Freedom* and *The Whorehouse* (also in German). He lives in Agoura, California, and belongs to NALC Branch 2902.

S.J. Rayner, age 64, lives in Ridge Manor, Florida, and is a 28-year veteran of the Postal Service. He is a retired member of NALC Branch 1071. Mr. Rayner has published stories in such journals as the *Lake Superior Review*, *New Infinity Review*, and *Greenfeather*.

Raymond Abney, age 40, lives in San Luis Obispo, California, and has worked for the Postal Service for 19 years. He is a member of NALC Branch 52.

Frank Criscenti, age 37, is an 11-year veteran of the Postal Service. He is a member of NALC Branch 1714 and lives in Redwood City, California.

Albert Nous is a retired letter carrier, age 78, and a member of NALC Branch 358. He lives in Mechanicville, New York, and worked for 30 years for the Postal Service.

Gene O'Neill, age 50, lives in Napa, California, and is a six-year veteran of the Postal Service. His stories have appeared in *Magazine of Science Fiction & Fantasy, Fantasy Book, Twilight Zone, Pulpsmith, Dragon,* and the French magazine *Fiction*. In 1980 he won the MDA/Jerry Lewis award for writing for his story "Big John", published in *Arise*. He is a member of NALC Branch 627.

Will Bevis, age 39, lives in Florence, Alabama, and has worked for the Postal Service for three years. He is a member of NALC Branch 892. He has published stories in *Blue and Gray* and *Retired Officer*.

Morris Weiss, age 75, is a 39-year retired veteran of the Postal Service and a member of NALC Branch 36 (New York). He now lives in Miami, Florida. Mr. Weiss has two previously published stories: "Uncle Harry" and "Down Under."

Irving Halpern, age 82, is a 30-year retired veteran of the Postal Service, a member of NALC Branch 41 (Brooklyn) and a member of NARFE Branch 139. He has previously published stories in the Miami Beach Sun Reporter. He now lives in Miami Beach.

Lee Peterson, age 42, has worked for the Postal Service for three years. He is a member of NALC Branch 28, and lives in Cottage Grove, Minnesota.

Frank Ware, age 35, has worked for the Postal Service for nine years and is a member of NALC Branch 1427. He lives in San Jose, California.